— William Shakespeare's —
The Tempest

adapted by **Daniel Conner**
illustrated by **Cynthia Martin**

Charles County Public Library
Potomac Branch
301-375-7375
www.ccplonline.org

visit us at
www.abdopublishing.com

Published by Magic Wagon, a division of the ABDO Publishing Group, 8000 West 78th Street, Edina, Minnesota 55439. Copyright © 2009 by Abdo Consulting Group, Inc. International copyrights reserved in all countries. All rights reserved. No part of this book may be reproduced in any form without written permission from the publisher.
Graphic Planet™ is a trademark and logo of Magic Wagon.

Printed in the United States.

Adapted by Daniel Conner
Illustrated by Cynthia Martin
Colors by Kelsey Shannon
Edited by Stephanie Hedlund and Rochelle Baltzer
Interior layout and design by Antarctic Press
Cover art by Cynthia Martin
Cover design by Neil Klinepier

Library of Congress Cataloging-in-Publication Data

Conner, Dan, 1985-
    William Shakespeare's The tempest / adapted by Daniel Conner ; illustrated by Cynthia Martin
        p. cm. -- (Graphic Shakespeare)
    Summary: Retells, in comic book format, Shakespeare's play about the exiled Duke of Milan who uses his magical powers to confront his enemies on an enchanted island.
    ISBN 978-1-60270-194-6
    1. Graphic novels. [1. Graphic novels. 2. Shakespeare, William, 1564-1616--Adaptations. 3. Youths' writings.] I. Martin, Cynthia, 1961- ill. II. Shakespeare, William, 1564-1616. Tempest. III. Title. IV. Title: Tempest.

PZ7.7.C66Wn 2008
741.5'973--dc22
                                                                    2008010746

Table of Contents

Cast of Characters

Alonso
King of Naples

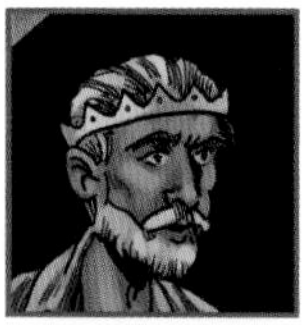

Ferdinand
Prince of Naples

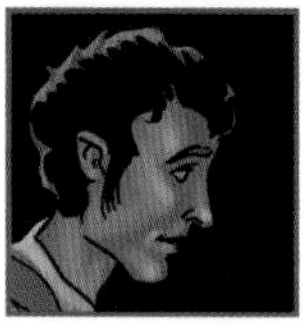

Sebastian
Brother of the king

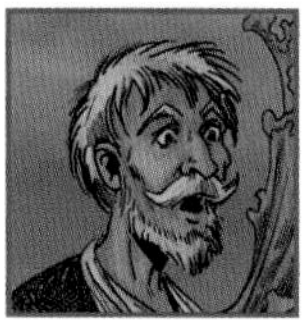

Gonzalo
Royal counselor

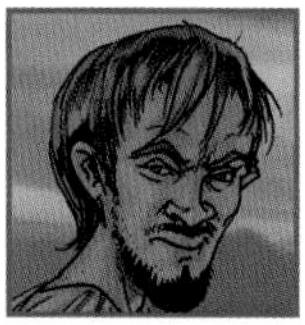

Antonio
Duke of Milan, brother of Prospero

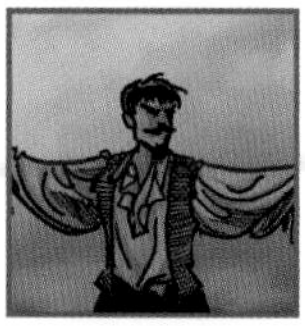

Trinculo
Court jester

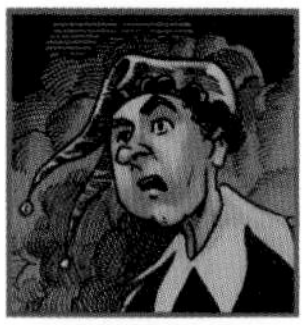

Stephano
Royal butler

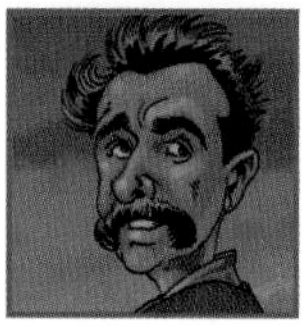

Master of the Ship

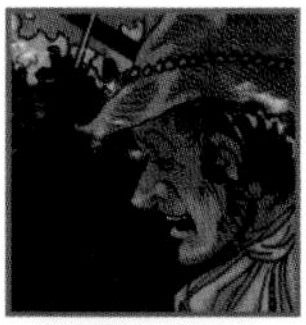

Boatswain

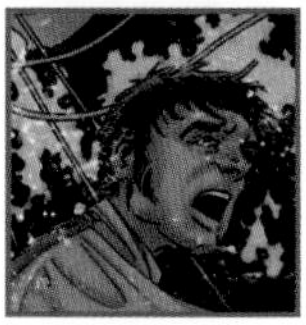

Prospero
Master of the island, sorcerer, former and rightful Duke of Milan

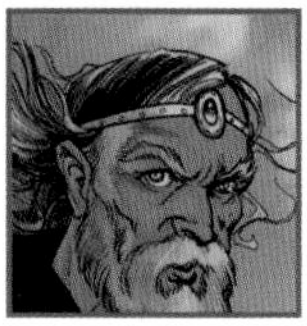

Miranda
Daughter of Prospero

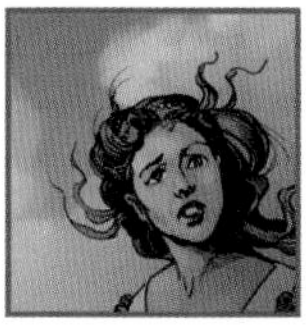

Ariel
Powerful spirit and slave to Prospero

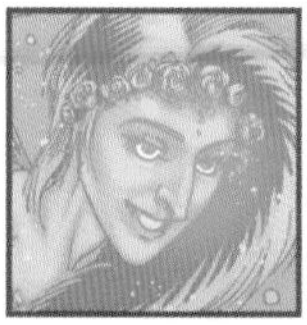

Caliban
Fishlike monster and slave to Prospero

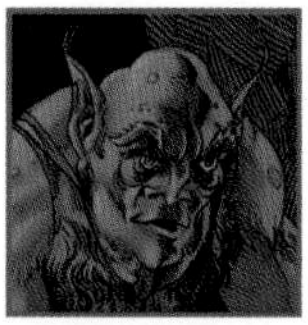

Sycorax
Former ruler of the island

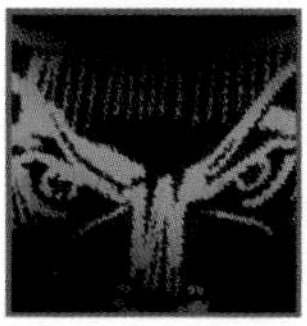

Our Setting

The Tempest is set on a mystical island near Italy, possibly in the Mediterranean Sea. The characters are from Italian cities of Milan and Naples. Both ancient cities were founded in 600 BC. They grew to be of great importance in Italy.

The mystical island has many different features, including "fresh springs, brine-pits, barren place and fertile." It also has ens, flats, bogs, and at least one area with no shelter. The people on the island can find berries, nuts, crab apples, and mussels to survive on.

It has been noticed that the characters in the play often see the island in different ways. This was part of the theme of Illusion Shakespeare was creating. This makes the island one of the major characters of *The Tempest*.

Act I

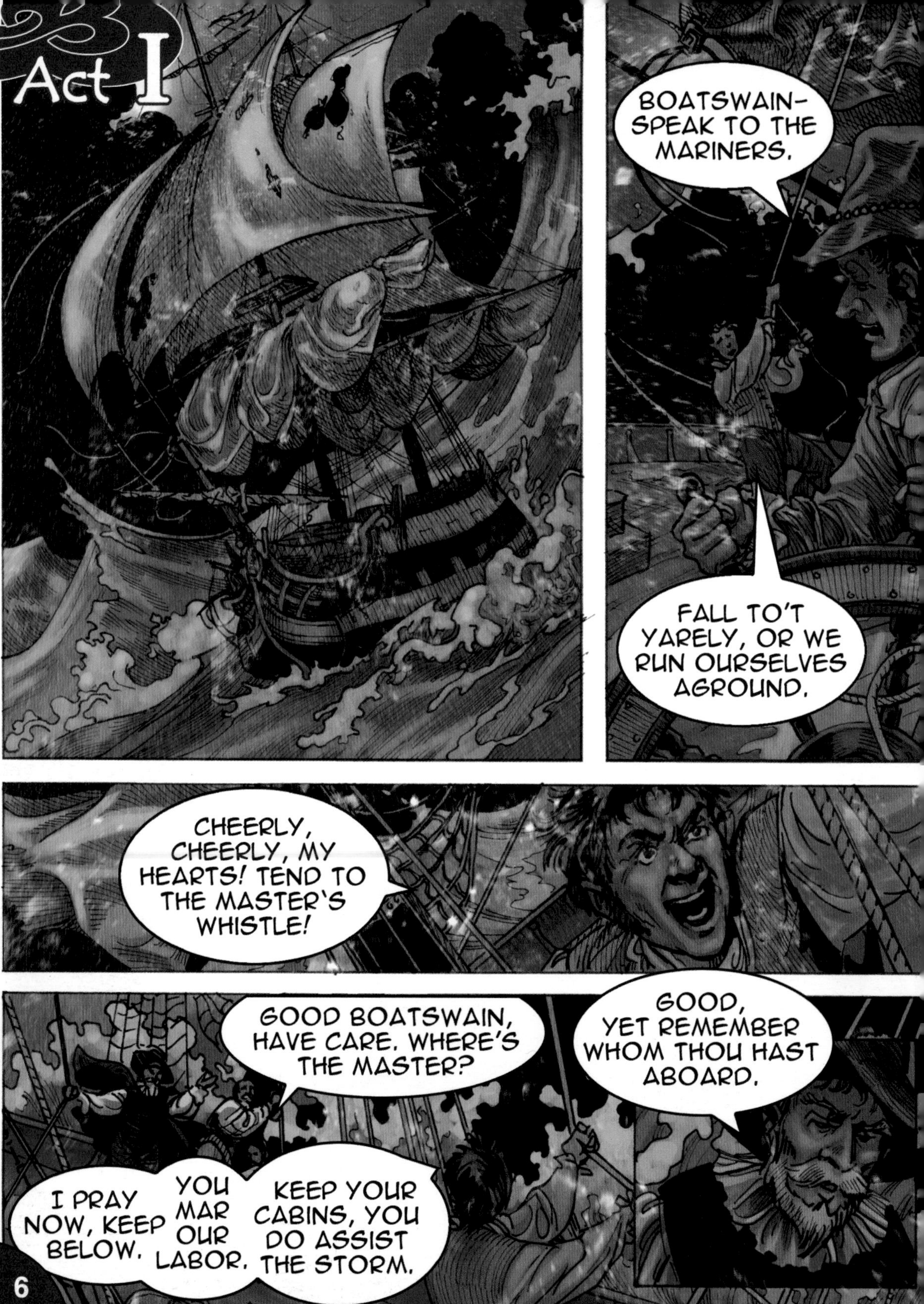
BOATSWAIN- SPEAK TO THE MARINERS.
FALL TO'T YARELY, OR WE RUN OURSELVES AGROUND.
CHEERLY, CHEERLY, MY HEARTS! TEND TO THE MASTER'S WHISTLE!
GOOD BOATSWAIN, HAVE CARE. WHERE'S THE MASTER?
I PRAY NOW, KEEP BELOW.
YOU MAR OUR LABOR.
KEEP YOUR CABINS, YOU DO ASSIST THE STORM.
GOOD, YET REMEMBER WHOM THOU HAST ABOARD.

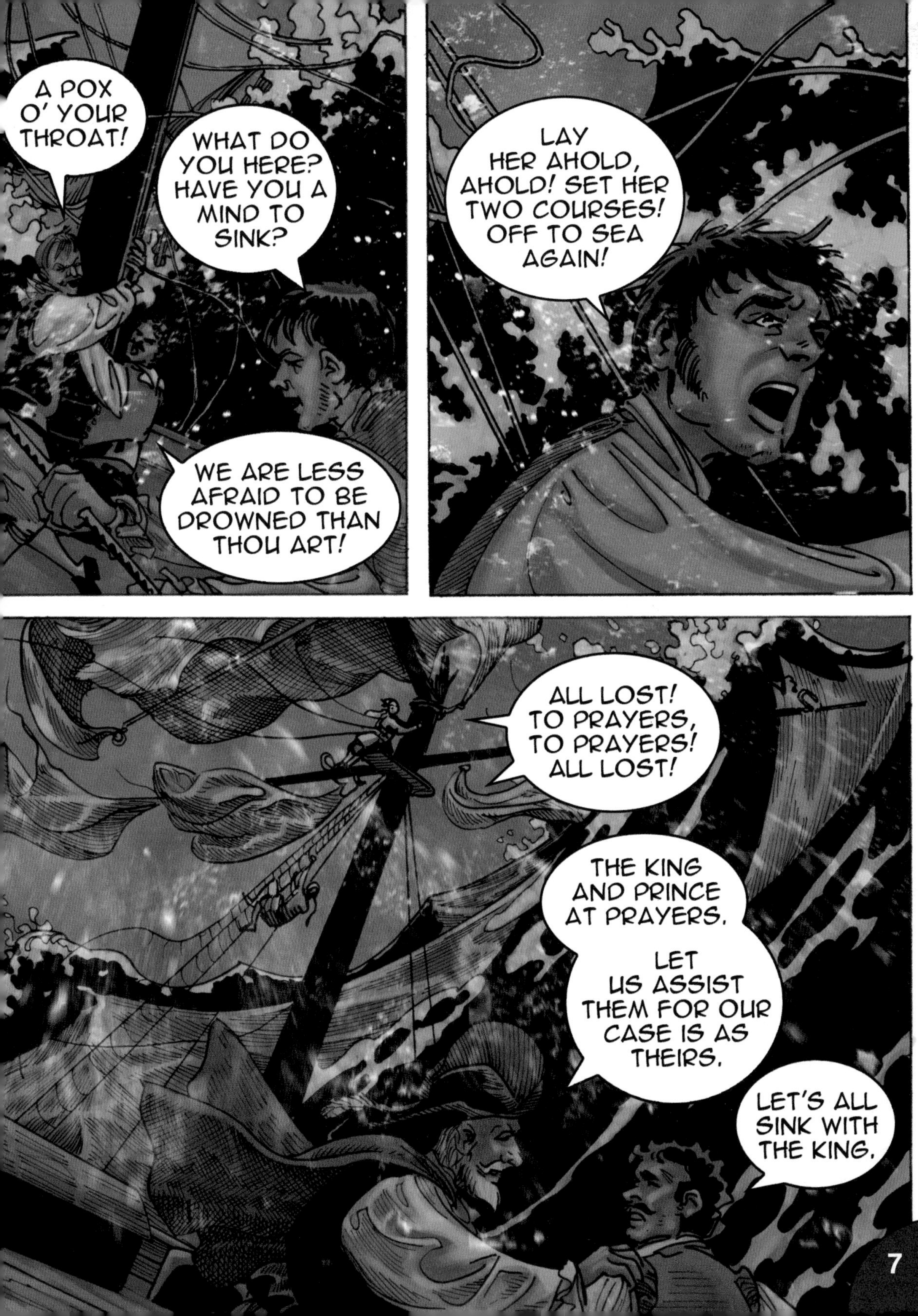
A POX O' YOUR THROAT!
WHAT DO YOU HERE? HAVE YOU A MIND TO SINK?
WE ARE LESS AFRAID TO BE DROWNED THAN THOU ART!
LAY HER AHOLD, AHOLD! SET HER TWO COURSES! OFF TO SEA AGAIN!
ALL LOST! TO PRAYERS, TO PRAYERS! ALL LOST!
THE KING AND PRINCE AT PRAYERS.
LET US ASSIST THEM FOR OUR CASE IS AS THEIRS.
LET'S ALL SINK WITH THE KING.

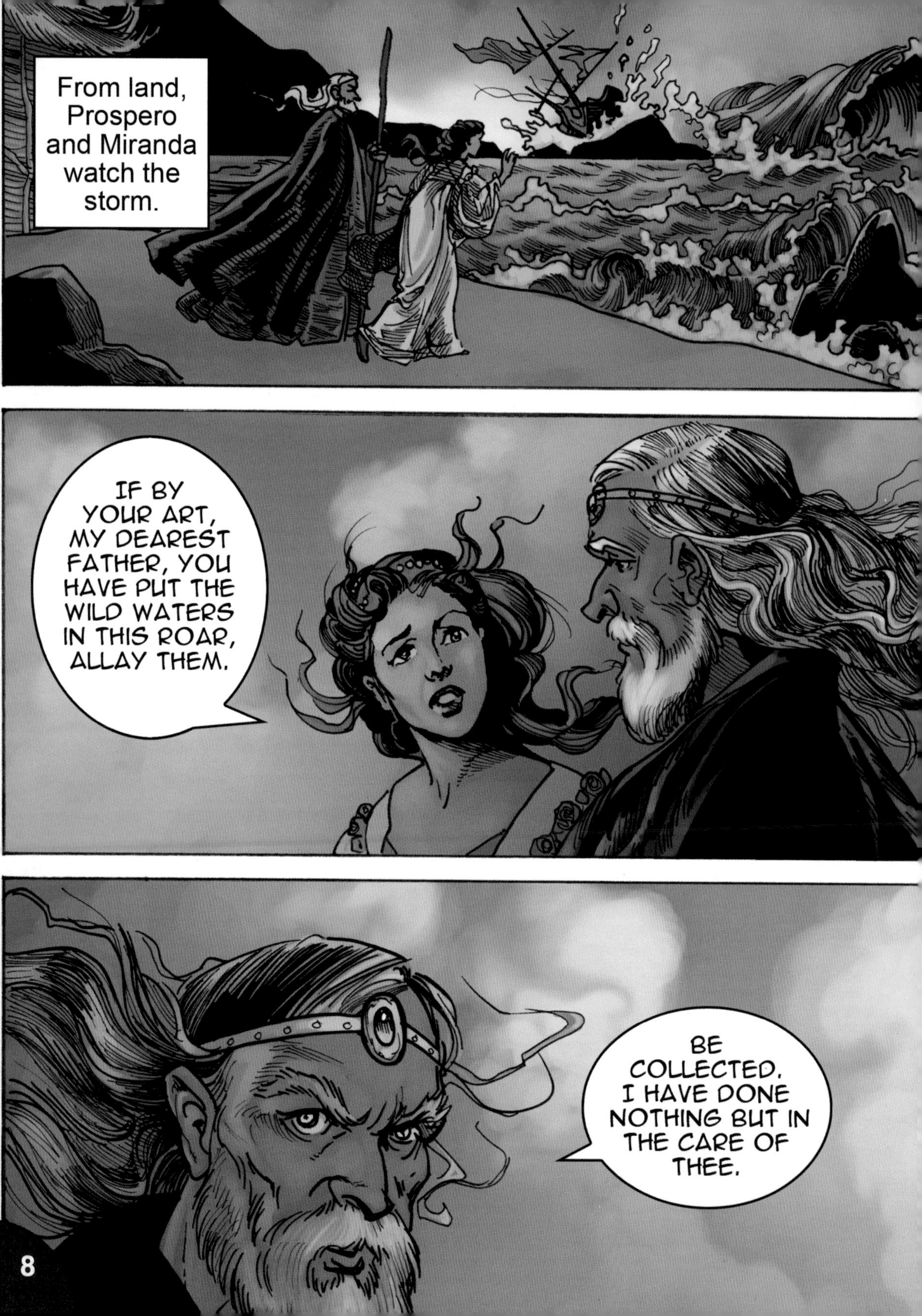
From land, Prospero and Miranda watch the storm.
IF BY YOUR ART, MY DEAREST FATHER, YOU HAVE PUT THE WILD WATERS IN THIS ROAR, ALLAY THEM.
BE COLLECTED. I HAVE DONE NOTHING BUT IN THE CARE OF THEE.

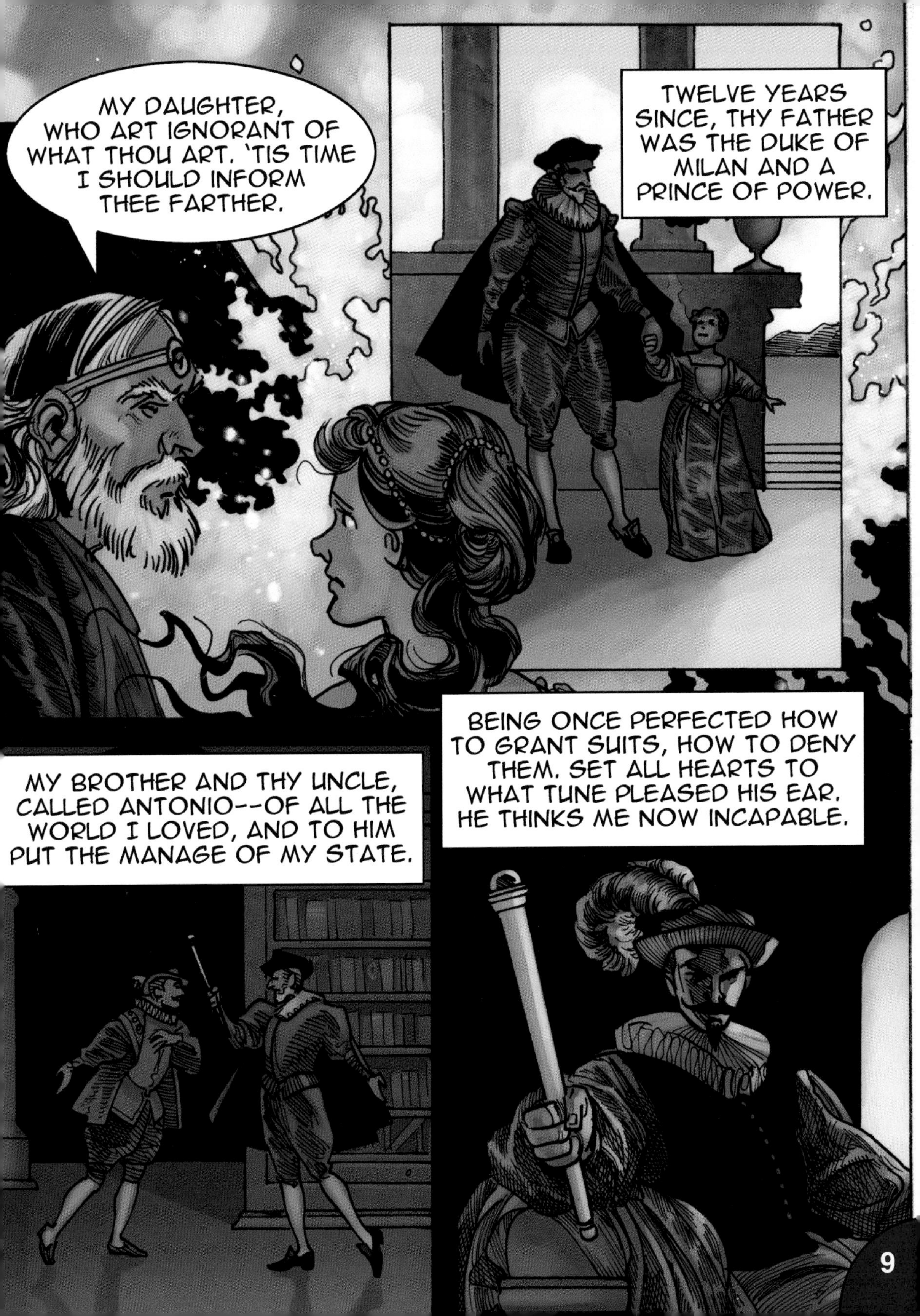
MY DAUGHTER, WHO ART IGNORANT OF WHAT THOU ART. 'TIS TIME I SHOULD INFORM THEE FARTHER.
TWELVE YEARS SINCE, THY FATHER WAS THE DUKE OF MILAN AND A PRINCE OF POWER.
MY BROTHER AND THY UNCLE, CALLED ANTONIO--OF ALL THE WORLD I LOVED, AND TO HIM PUT THE MANAGE OF MY STATE.
BEING ONCE PERFECTED HOW TO GRANT SUITS, HOW TO DENY THEM. SET ALL HEARTS TO WHAT TUNE PLEASED HIS EAR. HE THINKS ME NOW INCAPABLE.

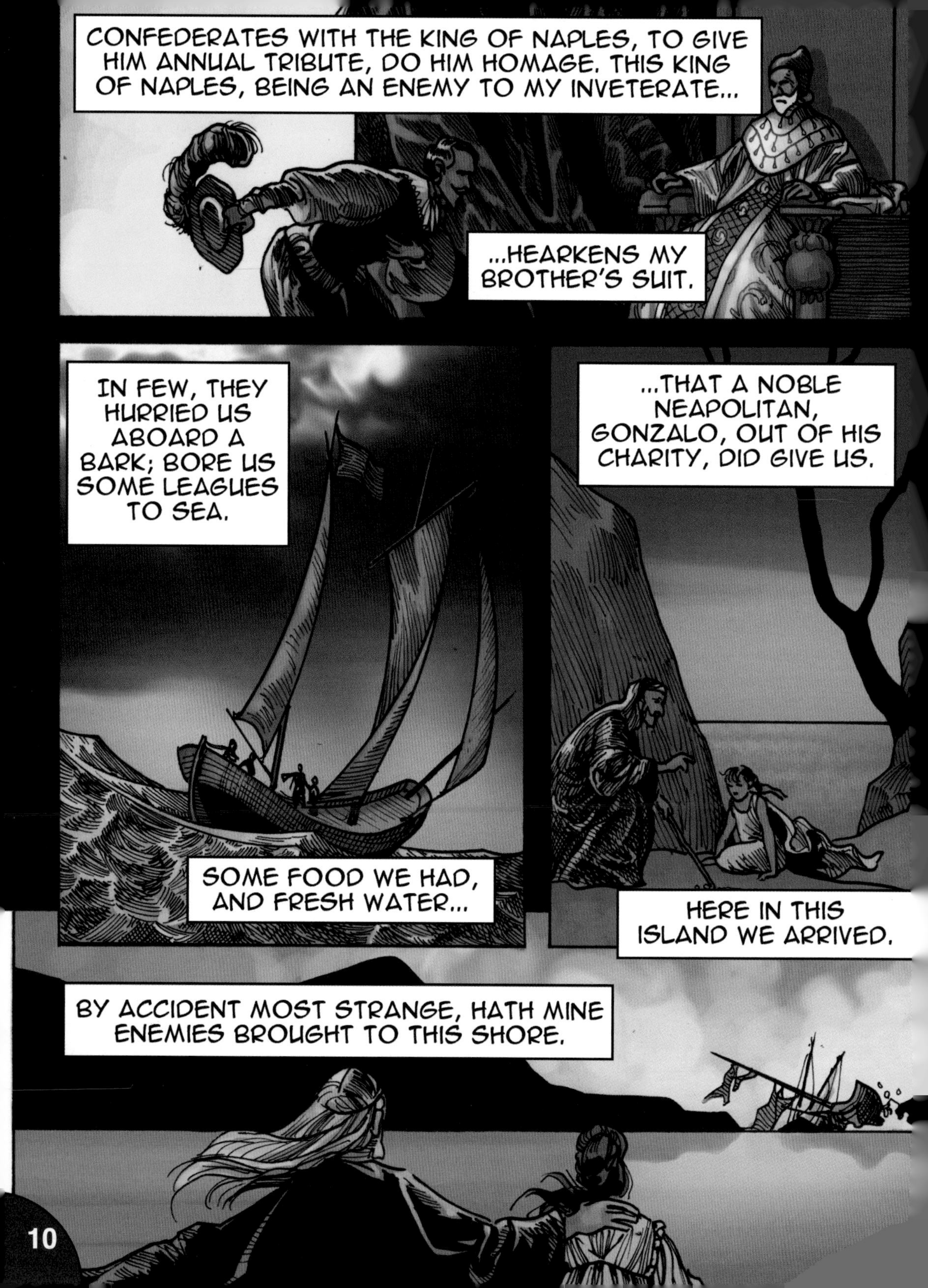
CONFEDERATES WITH THE KING OF NAPLES, TO GIVE HIM ANNUAL TRIBUTE, DO HIM HOMAGE. THIS KING OF NAPLES, BEING AN ENEMY TO MY INVETERATE...
...HEARKENS MY BROTHER'S SUIT.
IN FEW, THEY HURRIED US ABOARD A BARK; BORE US SOME LEAGUES TO SEA.
SOME FOOD WE HAD, AND FRESH WATER...
...THAT A NOBLE NEAPOLITAN, GONZALO, OUT OF HIS CHARITY, DID GIVE US.
HERE IN THIS ISLAND WE ARRIVED.
BY ACCIDENT MOST STRANGE, HATH MINE ENEMIES BROUGHT TO THIS SHORE.

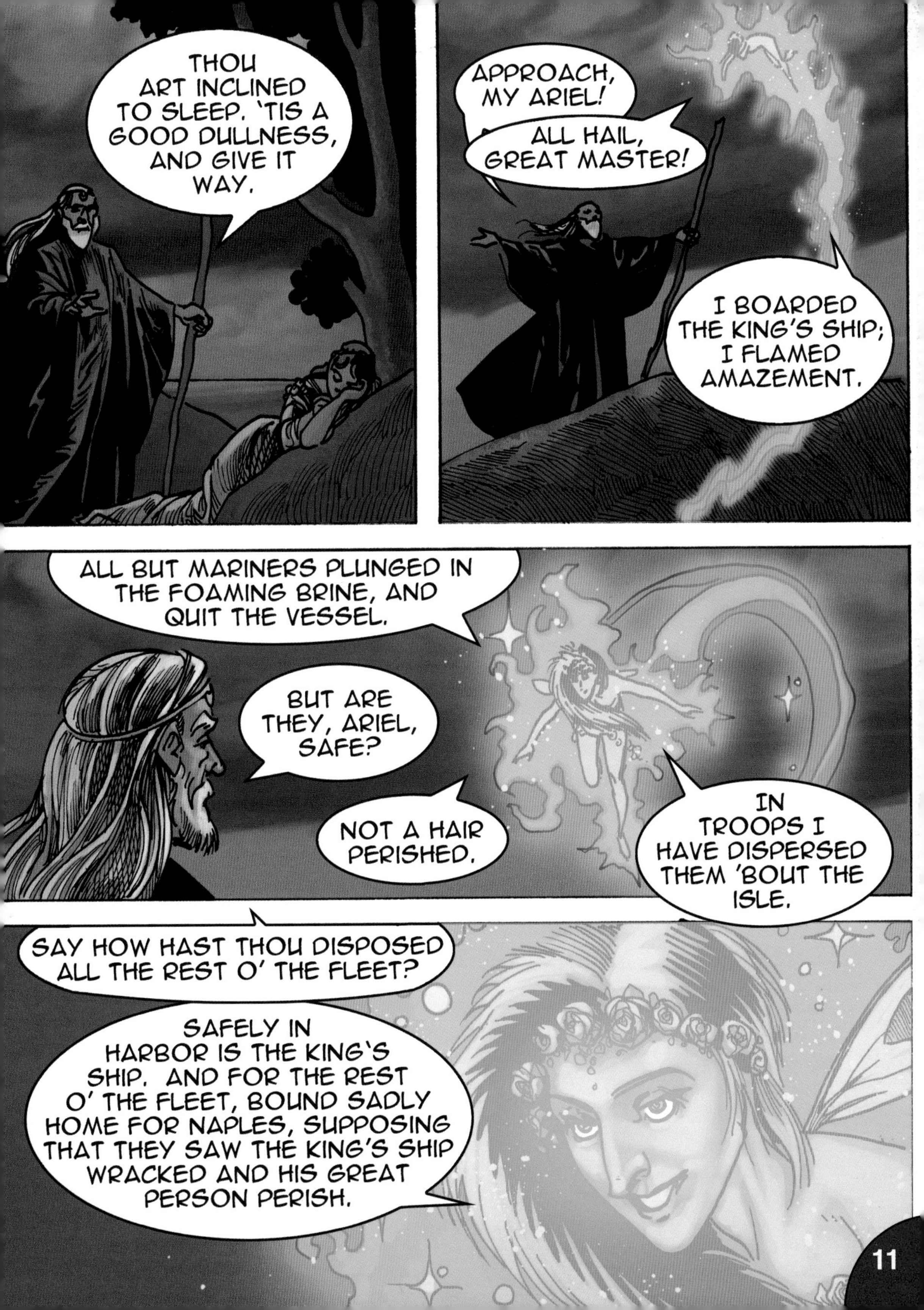
THOU ART INCLINED TO SLEEP. 'TIS A GOOD DULLNESS, AND GIVE IT WAY.
APPROACH, MY ARIEL!
ALL HAIL, GREAT MASTER!
I BOARDED THE KING'S SHIP; I FLAMED AMAZEMENT.
ALL BUT MARINERS PLUNGED IN THE FOAMING BRINE, AND QUIT THE VESSEL.
BUT ARE THEY, ARIEL, SAFE?
NOT A HAIR PERISHED.
IN TROOPS I HAVE DISPERSED THEM 'BOUT THE ISLE.
SAY HOW HAST THOU DISPOSED ALL THE REST O' THE FLEET?
SAFELY IN HARBOR IS THE KING'S SHIP. AND FOR THE REST O' THE FLEET, BOUND SADLY HOME FOR NAPLES, SUPPOSING THAT THEY SAW THE KING'S SHIP WRACKED AND HIS GREAT PERSON PERISH.

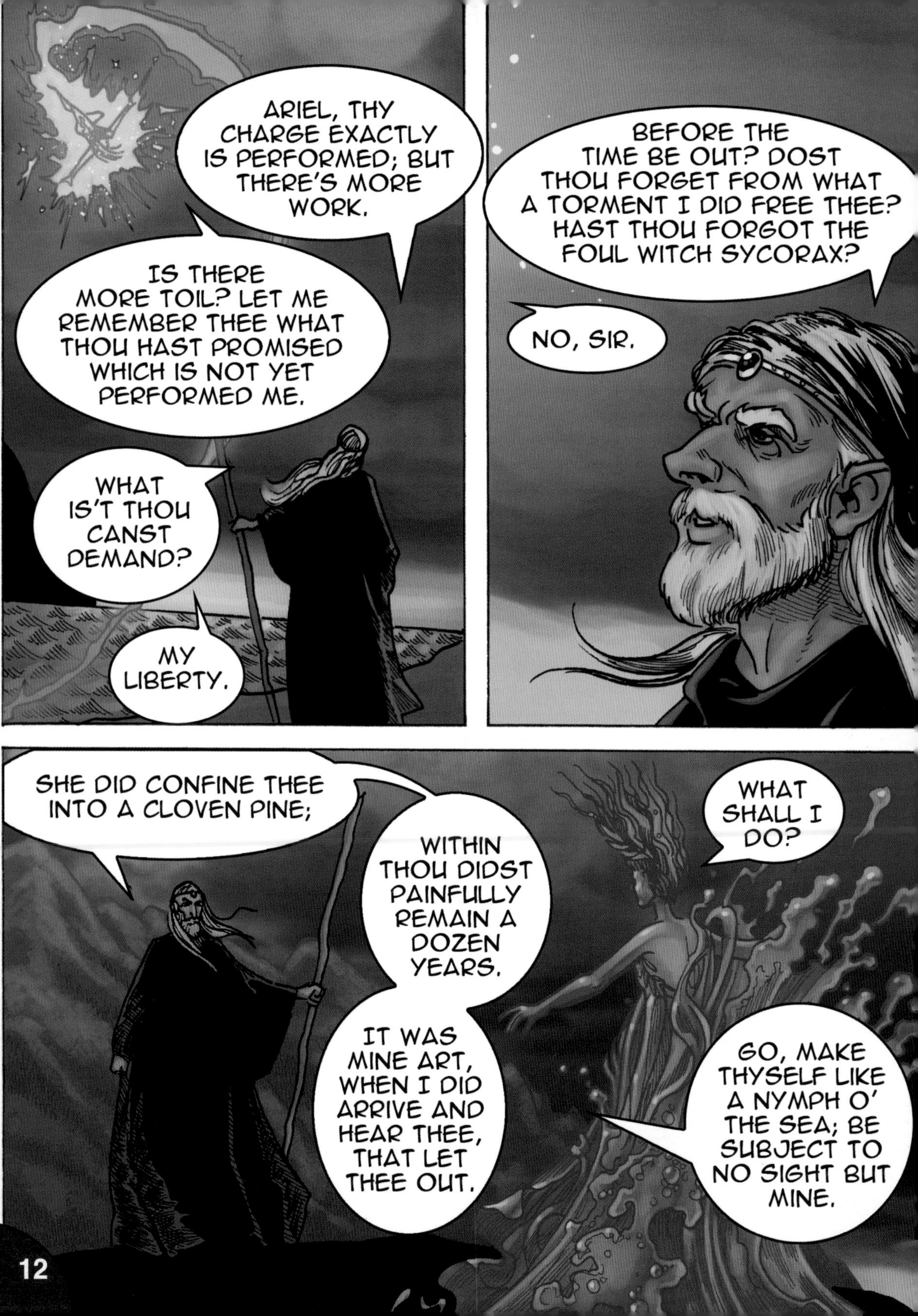
ARIEL, THY CHARGE EXACTLY IS PERFORMED; BUT THERE'S MORE WORK.
IS THERE MORE TOIL? LET ME REMEMBER THEE WHAT THOU HAST PROMISED WHICH IS NOT YET PERFORMED ME.
WHAT IS'T THOU CANST DEMAND?
MY LIBERTY.
BEFORE THE TIME BE OUT? DOST THOU FORGET FROM WHAT A TORMENT I DID FREE THEE? HAST THOU FORGOT THE FOUL WITCH SYCORAX?
NO, SIR.
SHE DID CONFINE THEE INTO A CLOVEN PINE;
WITHIN THOU DIDST PAINFULLY REMAIN A DOZEN YEARS.
IT WAS MINE ART, WHEN I DID ARRIVE AND HEAR THEE, THAT LET THEE OUT.
WHAT SHALL I DO?
GO, MAKE THYSELF LIKE A NYMPH O' THE SEA; BE SUBJECT TO NO SIGHT BUT MINE.

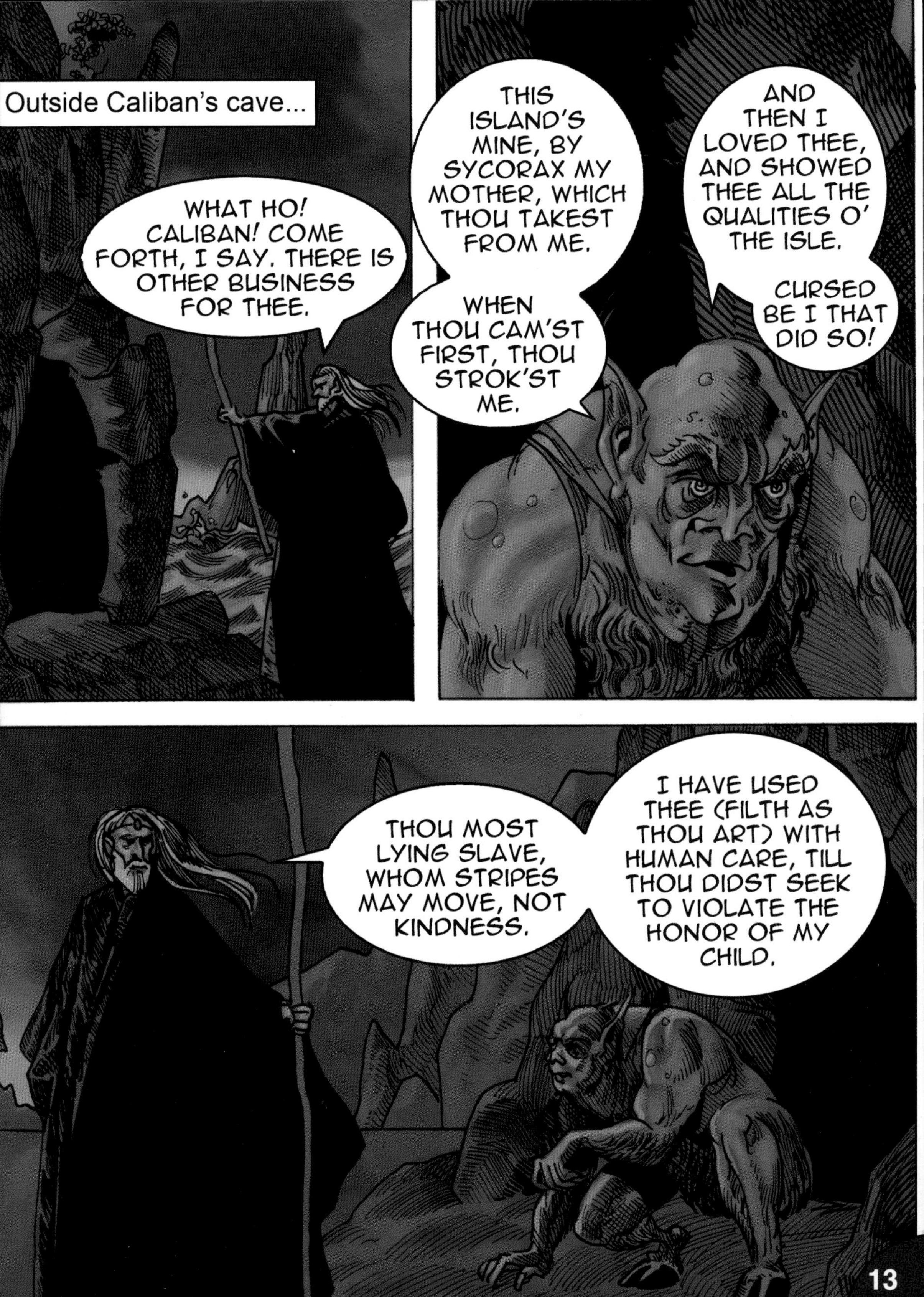
Outside Caliban's cave...
WHAT HO! CALIBAN! COME FORTH, I SAY. THERE IS OTHER BUSINESS FOR THEE.
THIS ISLAND'S MINE, BY SYCORAX MY MOTHER, WHICH THOU TAKEST FROM ME.
WHEN THOU CAM'ST FIRST, THOU STROK'ST ME.
AND THEN I LOVED THEE, AND SHOWED THEE ALL THE QUALITIES O' THE ISLE.
CURSED BE I THAT DID SO!
THOU MOST LYING SLAVE, WHOM STRIPES MAY MOVE, NOT KINDNESS.
I HAVE USED THEE (FILTH AS THOU ART) WITH HUMAN CARE, TILL THOU DIDST SEEK TO VIOLATE THE HONOR OF MY CHILD.

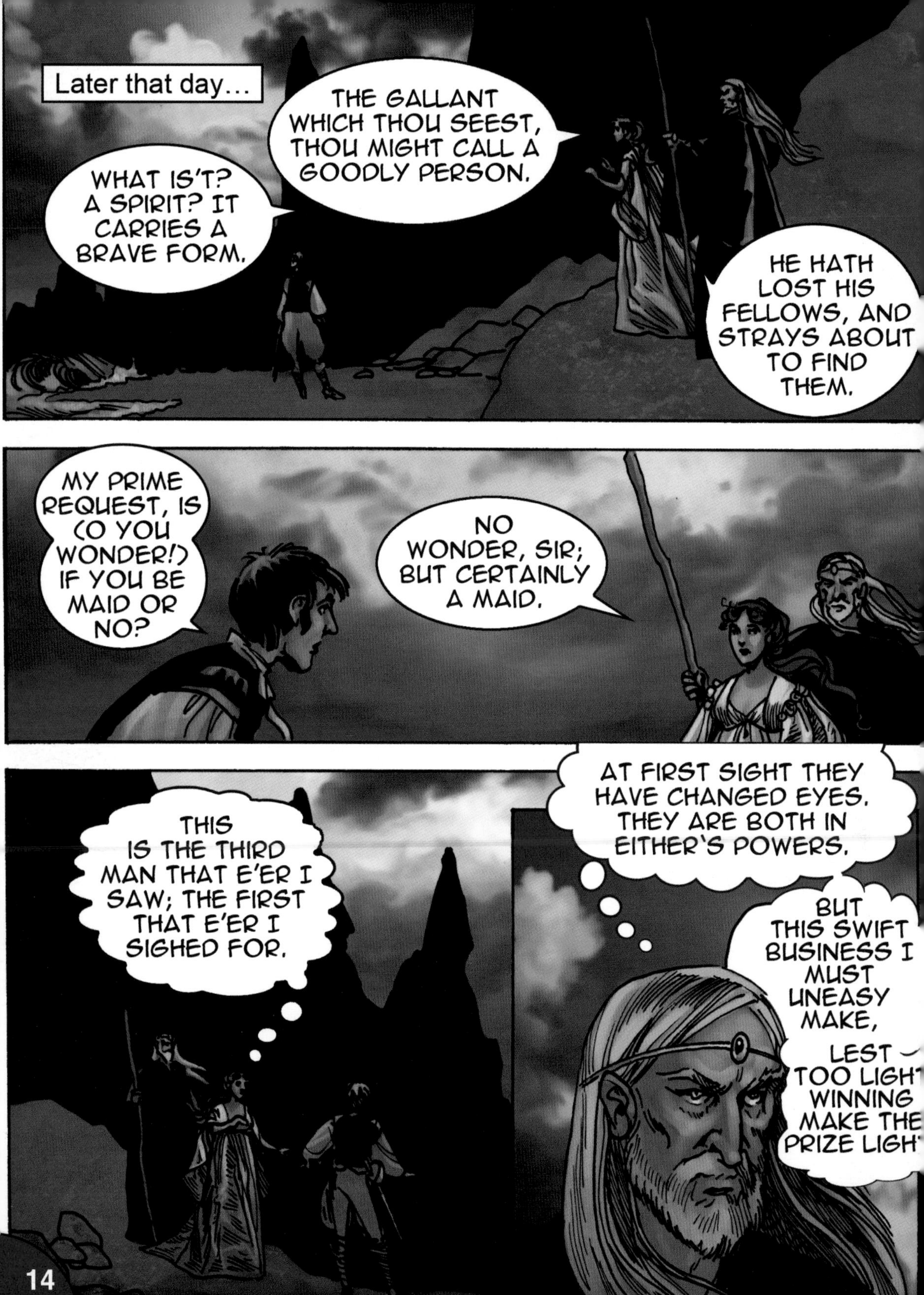

Later that day…
WHAT IS'T? A SPIRIT? IT CARRIES A BRAVE FORM.
THE GALLANT WHICH THOU SEEST, THOU MIGHT CALL A GOODLY PERSON.
HE HATH LOST HIS FELLOWS, AND STRAYS ABOUT TO FIND THEM.
MY PRIME REQUEST, IS (O YOU WONDER!) IF YOU BE MAID OR NO?
NO WONDER, SIR; BUT CERTAINLY A MAID.
THIS IS THE THIRD MAN THAT E'ER I SAW; THE FIRST THAT E'ER I SIGHED FOR.
AT FIRST SIGHT THEY HAVE CHANGED EYES. THEY ARE BOTH IN EITHER'S POWERS.
BUT THIS SWIFT BUSINESS I MUST UNEASY MAKE,
LEST TOO LIGH WINNING MAKE THE PRIZE LIGH

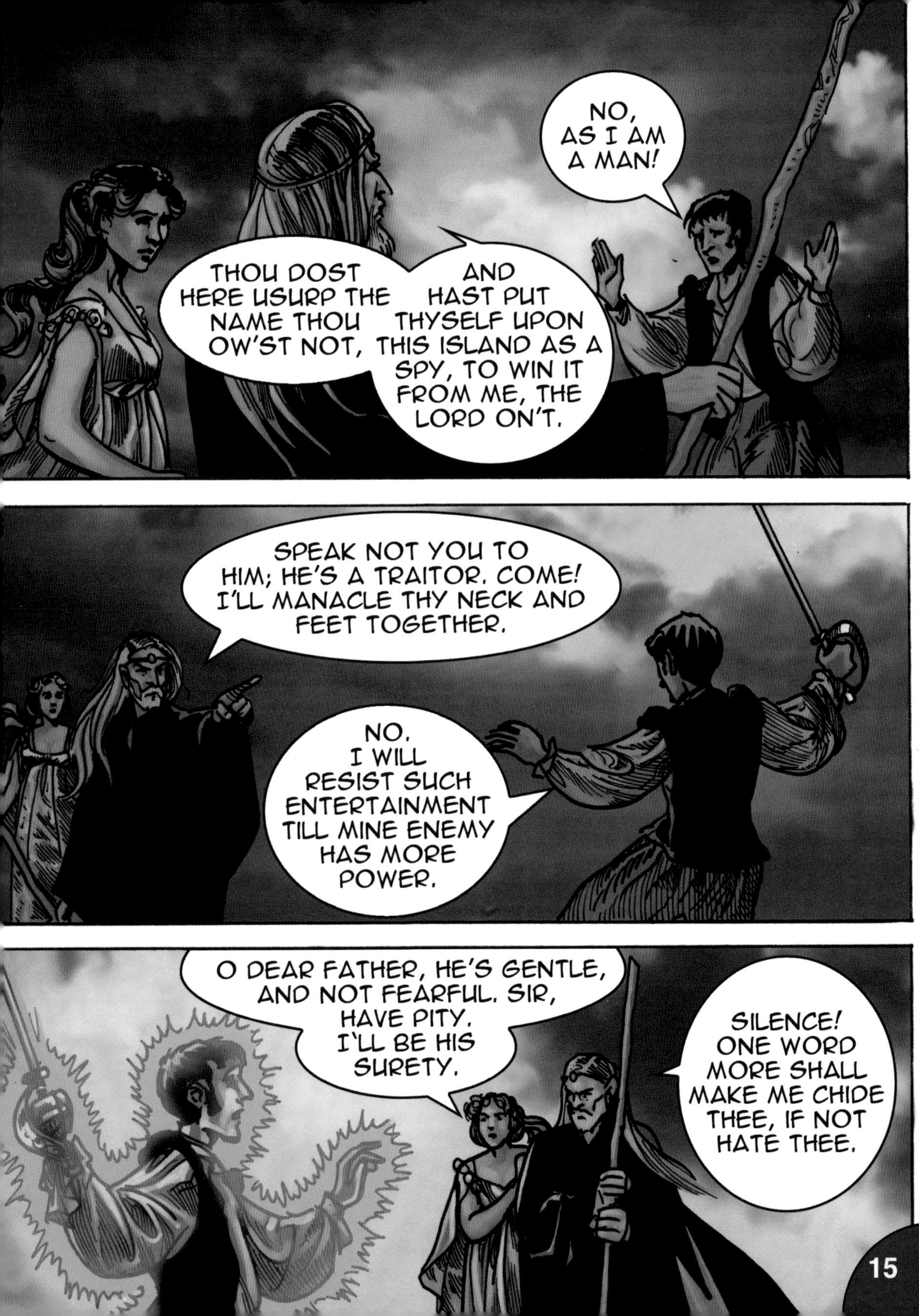

NO, AS I AM A MAN!
THOU DOST HERE USURP THE NAME THOU OW'ST NOT,
AND HAST PUT THYSELF UPON THIS ISLAND AS A SPY, TO WIN IT FROM ME, THE LORD ON'T.
SPEAK NOT YOU TO HIM; HE'S A TRAITOR. COME! I'LL MANACLE THY NECK AND FEET TOGETHER.
NO. I WILL RESIST SUCH ENTERTAINMENT TILL MINE ENEMY HAS MORE POWER.
O DEAR FATHER, HE'S GENTLE, AND NOT FEARFUL. SIR, HAVE PITY. I'LL BE HIS SURETY.
SILENCE! ONE WORD MORE SHALL MAKE ME CHIDE THEE, IF NOT HATE THEE.

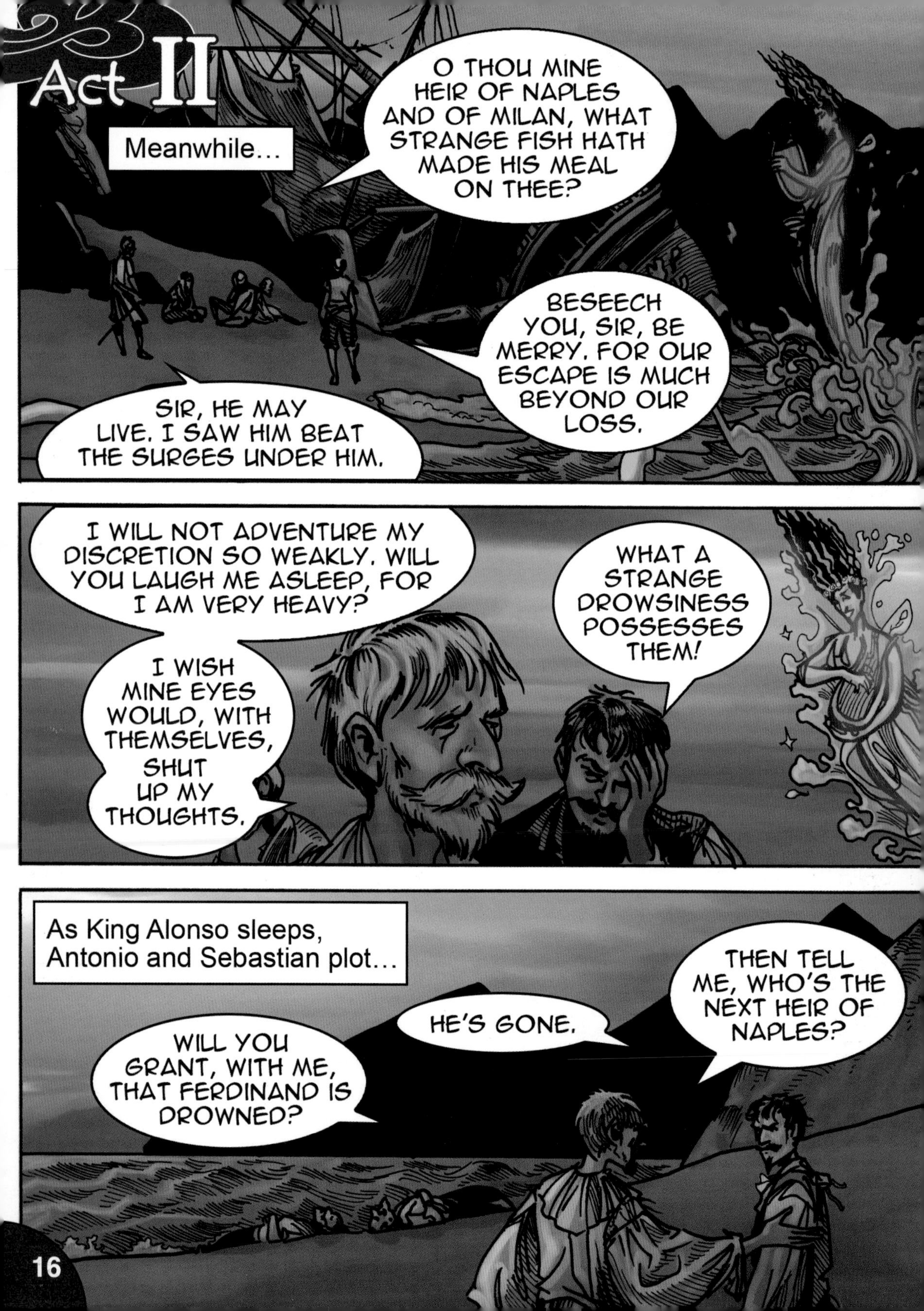
Act II
Meanwhile…
O THOU MINE HEIR OF NAPLES AND OF MILAN, WHAT STRANGE FISH HATH MADE HIS MEAL ON THEE?
BESEECH YOU, SIR, BE MERRY. FOR OUR ESCAPE IS MUCH BEYOND OUR LOSS.
SIR, HE MAY LIVE. I SAW HIM BEAT THE SURGES UNDER HIM.
I WILL NOT ADVENTURE MY DISCRETION SO WEAKLY. WILL YOU LAUGH ME ASLEEP, FOR I AM VERY HEAVY?
I WISH MINE EYES WOULD, WITH THEMSELVES, SHUT UP MY THOUGHTS.
WHAT A STRANGE DROWSINESS POSSESSES THEM!
As King Alonso sleeps, Antonio and Sebastian plot…
WILL YOU GRANT, WITH ME, THAT FERDINAND IS DROWNED?
HE'S GONE.
THEN TELL ME, WHO'S THE NEXT HEIR OF NAPLES?

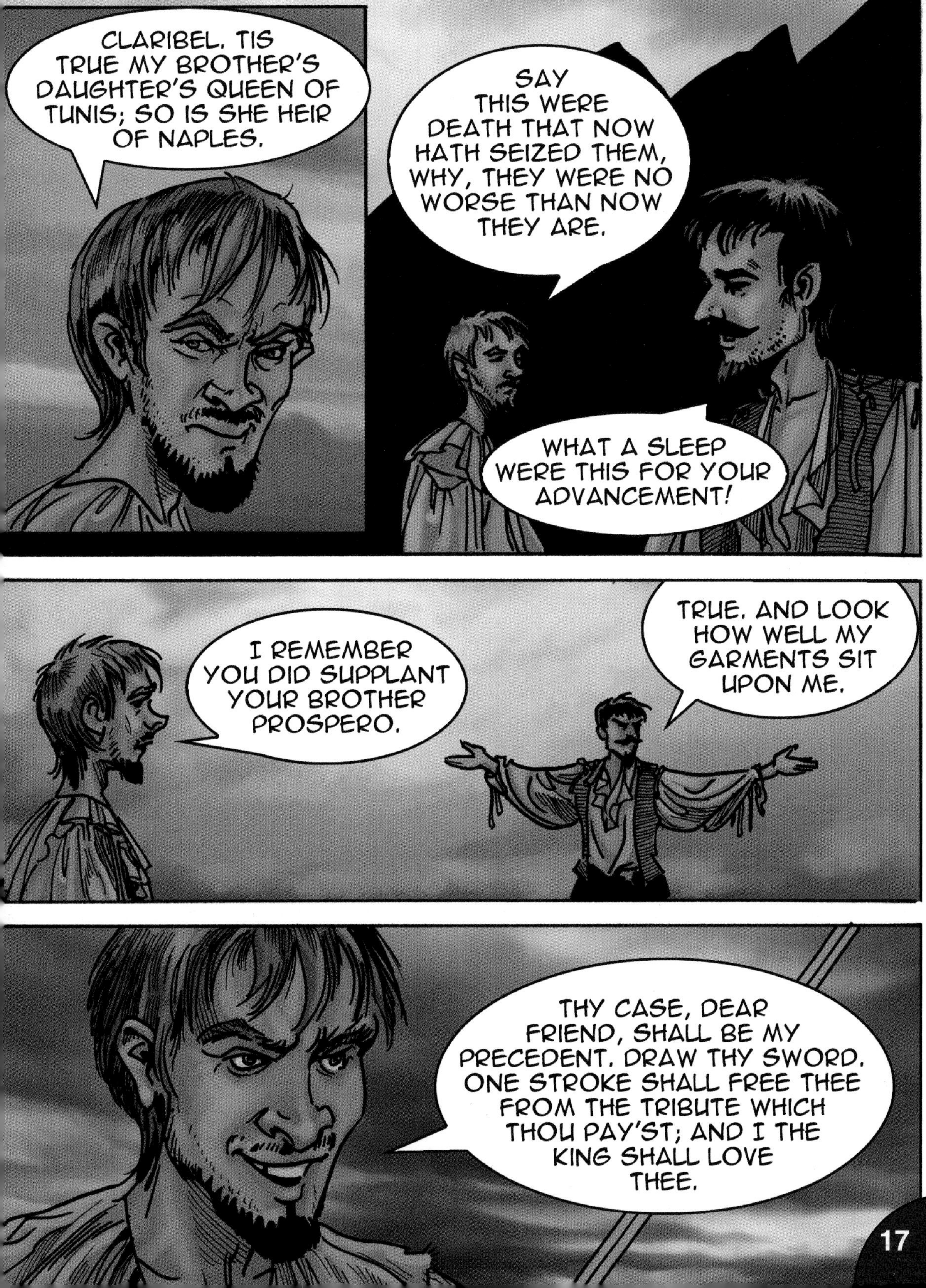

CLARIBEL. TIS TRUE MY BROTHER'S DAUGHTER'S QUEEN OF TUNIS; SO IS SHE HEIR OF NAPLES.
SAY THIS WERE DEATH THAT NOW HATH SEIZED THEM, WHY, THEY WERE NO WORSE THAN NOW THEY ARE.
WHAT A SLEEP WERE THIS FOR YOUR ADVANCEMENT!
I REMEMBER YOU DID SUPPLANT YOUR BROTHER PROSPERO.
TRUE. AND LOOK HOW WELL MY GARMENTS SIT UPON ME.
THY CASE, DEAR FRIEND, SHALL BE MY PRECEDENT. DRAW THY SWORD. ONE STROKE SHALL FREE THEE FROM THE TRIBUTE WHICH THOU PAY'ST; AND I THE KING SHALL LOVE THEE.

IF OF LIFE YOU KEEP A CARE, SHAKE OFF SLUMBER, AND BEWARE. AWAKE, AWAKE!

NOW, GOOD ANGELS PRESERVE THE KING!

WHY, HOW NOW? WHY ARE YOU DRAWN?

WE HEARD A HOLLOW BURST OF BELLOWING LIKE BULLS, OR RATHER LIONS.

DID'T NOT WAKE YOU?

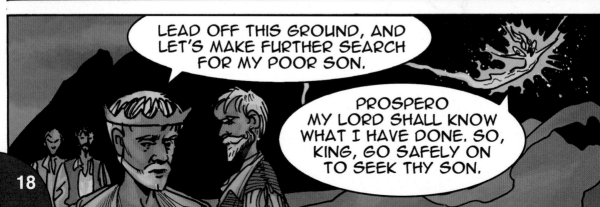

LEAD OFF THIS GROUND, AND LET'S MAKE FURTHER SEARCH FOR MY POOR SON.

PROSPERO MY LORD SHALL KNOW WHAT I HAVE DONE. SO, KING, GO SAFELY ON TO SEEK THY SON.

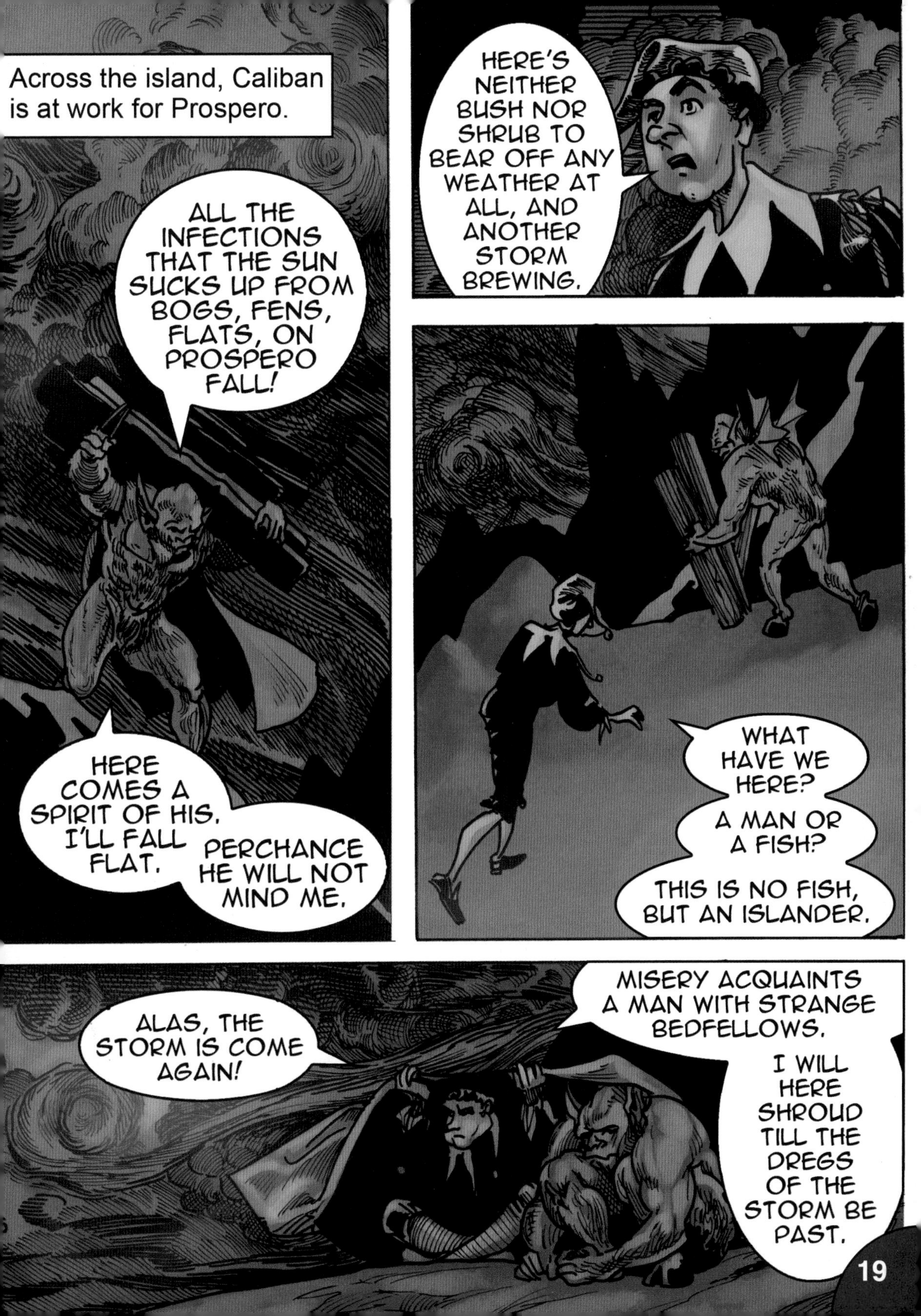

Across the island, Caliban is at work for Prospero.
ALL THE INFECTIONS THAT THE SUN SUCKS UP FROM BOGS, FENS, FLATS, ON PROSPERO FALL!
HERE COMES A SPIRIT OF HIS. I'LL FALL FLAT.
PERCHANCE HE WILL NOT MIND ME.
HERE'S NEITHER BUSH NOR SHRUB TO BEAR OFF ANY WEATHER AT ALL, AND ANOTHER STORM BREWING.
WHAT HAVE WE HERE?
A MAN OR A FISH?
THIS IS NO FISH, BUT AN ISLANDER.
ALAS, THE STORM IS COME AGAIN!
MISERY ACQUAINTS A MAN WITH STRANGE BEDFELLOWS.
I WILL HERE SHROUD TILL THE DREGS OF THE STORM BE PAST.

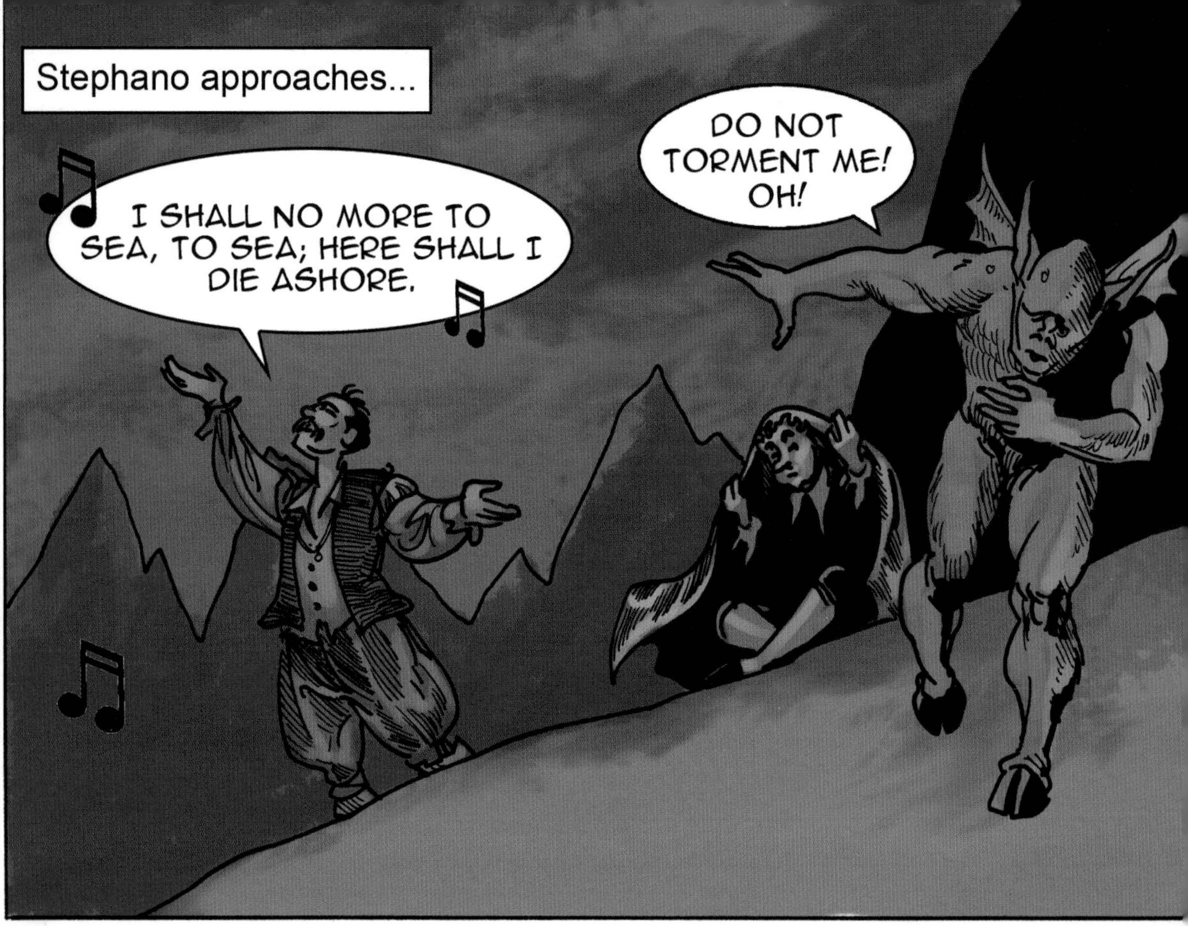
Stephano approaches...
I SHALL NO MORE TO SEA, TO SEA; HERE SHALL I DIE ASHORE.
DO NOT TORMENT ME! OH!

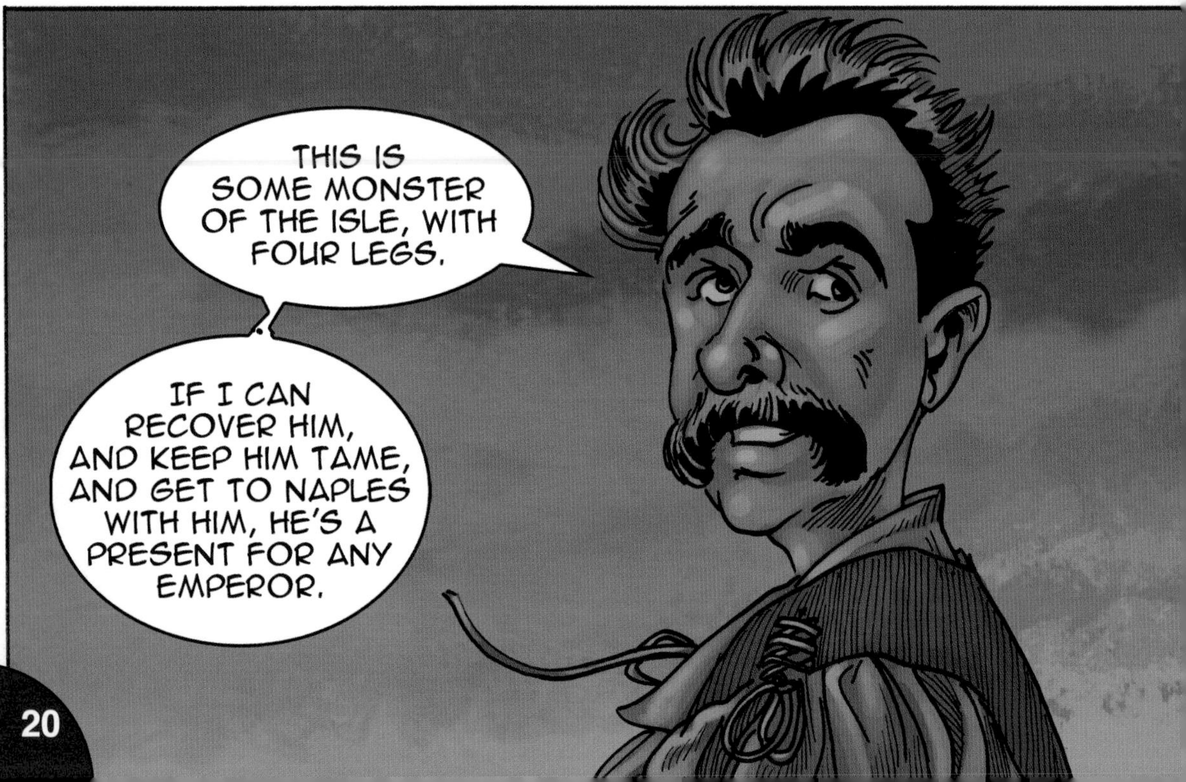
THIS IS SOME MONSTER OF THE ISLE, WITH FOUR LEGS.
IF I CAN RECOVER HIM, AND KEEP HIM TAME, AND GET TO NAPLES WITH HIM, HE'S A PRESENT FOR ANY EMPEROR.

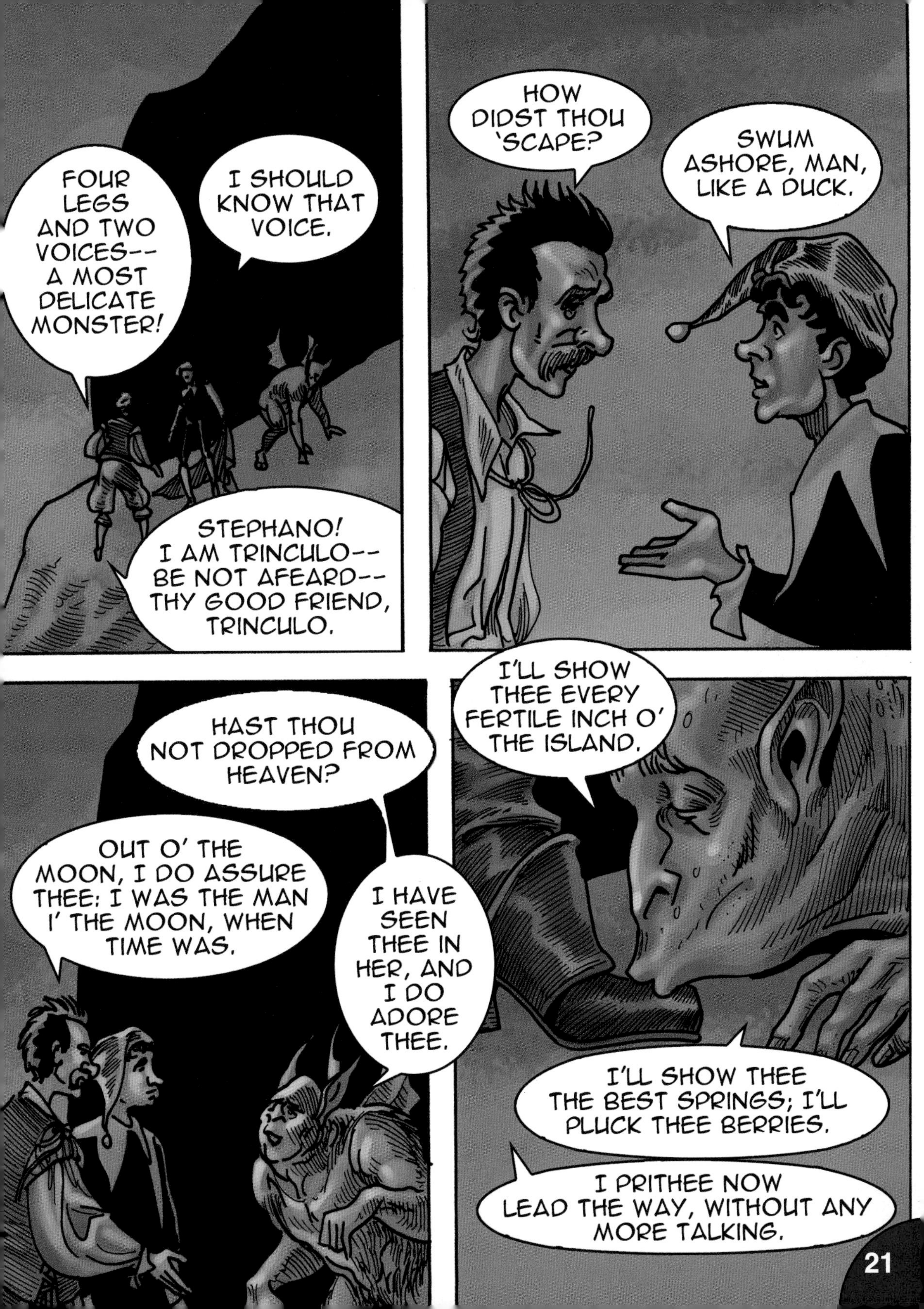
FOUR LEGS AND TWO VOICES-- A MOST DELICATE MONSTER!
I SHOULD KNOW THAT VOICE.
STEPHANO! I AM TRINCULO-- BE NOT AFEARD-- THY GOOD FRIEND, TRINCULO.
HOW DIDST THOU 'SCAPE?
SWUM ASHORE, MAN, LIKE A DUCK.
HAST THOU NOT DROPPED FROM HEAVEN?
OUT O' THE MOON, I DO ASSURE THEE: I WAS THE MAN I' THE MOON, WHEN TIME WAS.
I HAVE SEEN THEE IN HER, AND I DO ADORE THEE.
I'LL SHOW THEE EVERY FERTILE INCH O' THE ISLAND.
I'LL SHOW THEE THE BEST SPRINGS; I'LL PLUCK THEE BERRIES.
I PRITHEE NOW LEAD THE WAY, WITHOUT ANY MORE TALKING.

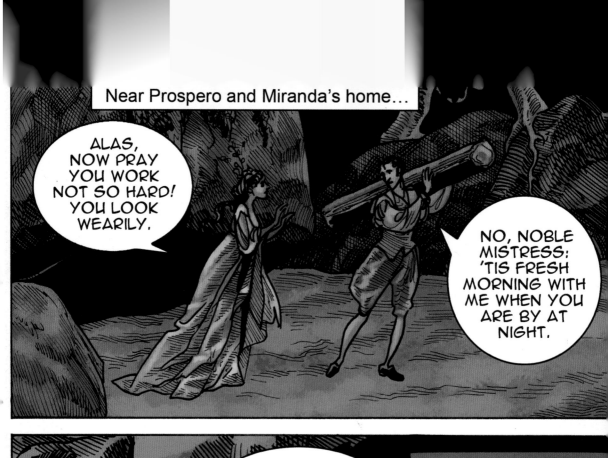

Near Prospero and Miranda's home…

ALAS, NOW PRAY YOU WORK NOT SO HARD! YOU LOOK WEARILY.

NO, NOBLE MISTRESS: 'TIS FRESH MORNING WITH ME WHEN YOU ARE BY AT NIGHT.

I WOULD NOT WISH ANY COMPANION IN THE WORLD BUT YOU.

I AM A PRINCE, MIRANDA; I DO THINK, A KING. THE VERY INSTANT I SAW YOU, MY HEART FLEW TO YOUR SERVICE.

DO YOU LOVE ME?

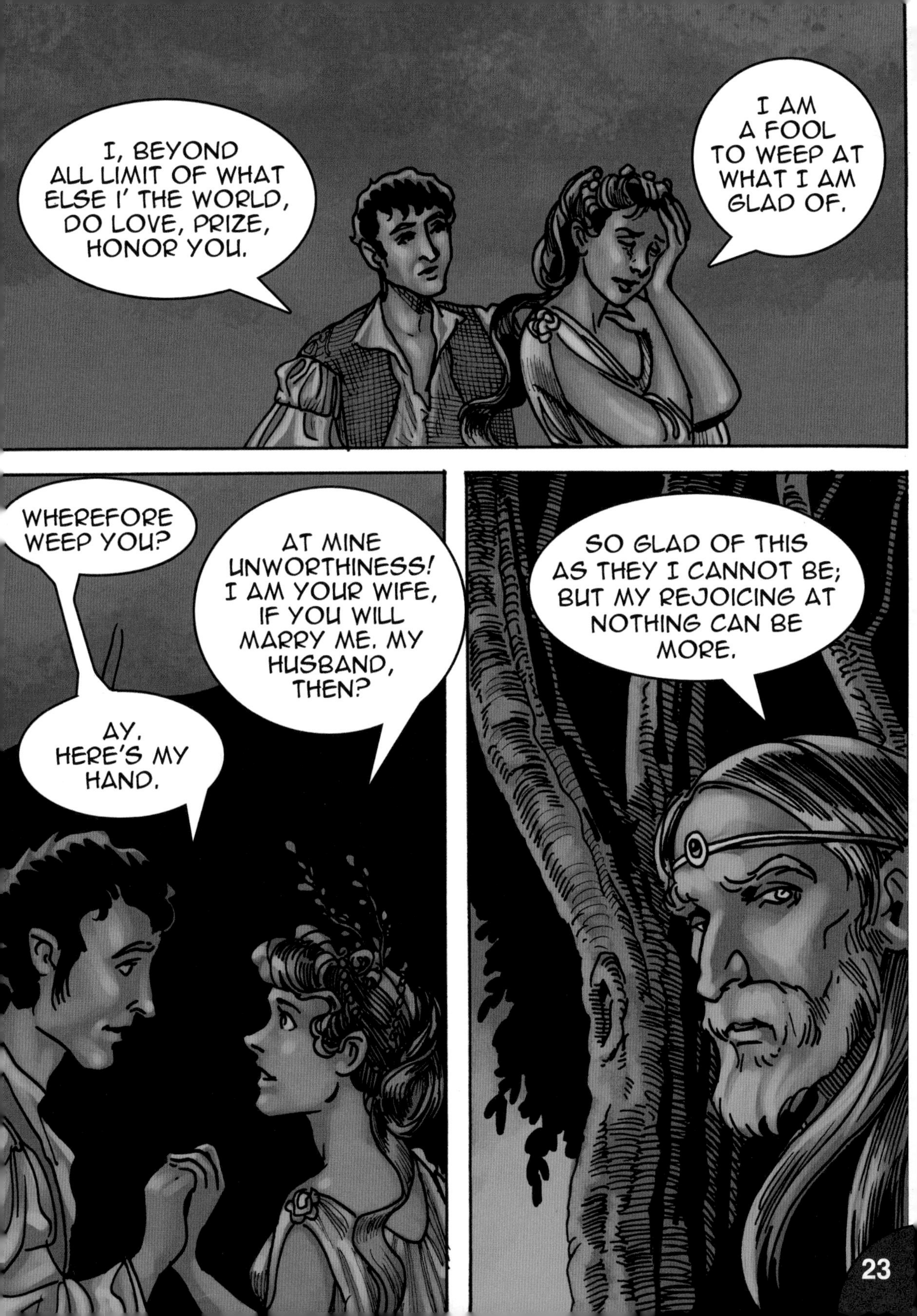
I, BEYOND ALL LIMIT OF WHAT ELSE I' THE WORLD, DO LOVE, PRIZE, HONOR YOU.
I AM A FOOL TO WEEP AT WHAT I AM GLAD OF.
WHEREFORE WEEP YOU?
AT MINE UNWORTHINESS! I AM YOUR WIFE, IF YOU WILL MARRY ME. MY HUSBAND, THEN?
AY. HERE'S MY HAND.
SO GLAD OF THIS AS THEY I CANNOT BE; BUT MY REJOICING AT NOTHING CAN BE MORE.

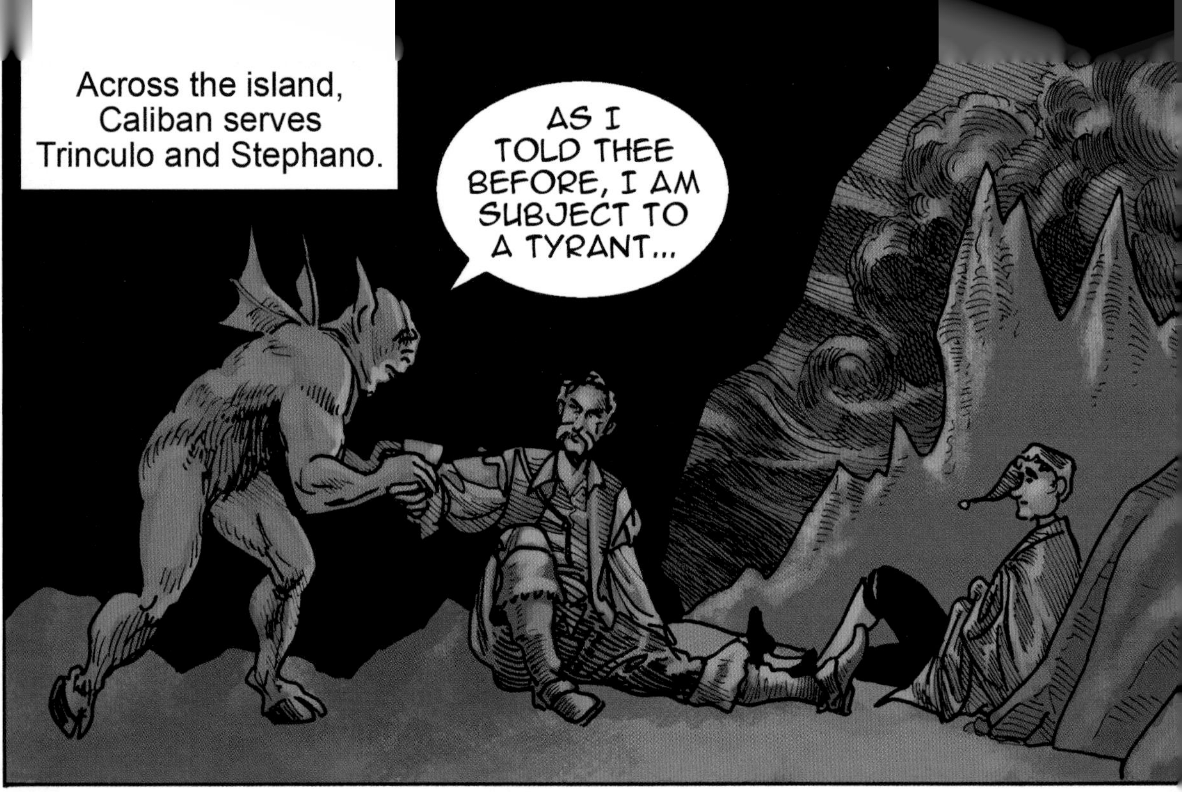
Across the island, Caliban serves Trinculo and Stephano.
AS I TOLD THEE BEFORE, I AM SUBJECT TO A TYRANT...

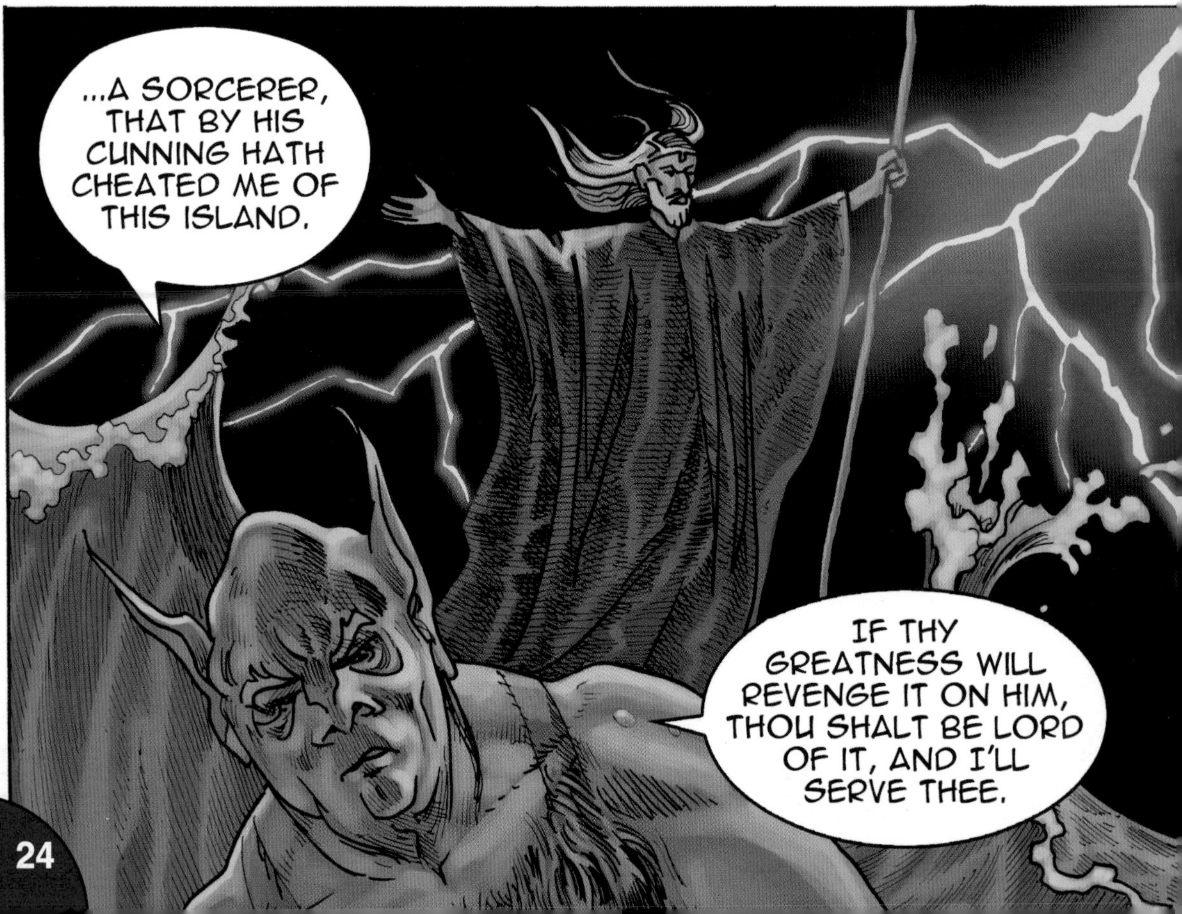
...A SORCERER, THAT BY HIS CUNNING HATH CHEATED ME OF THIS ISLAND.
IF THY GREATNESS WILL REVENGE IT ON HIM, THOU SHALT BE LORD OF IT, AND I'LL SERVE THEE.

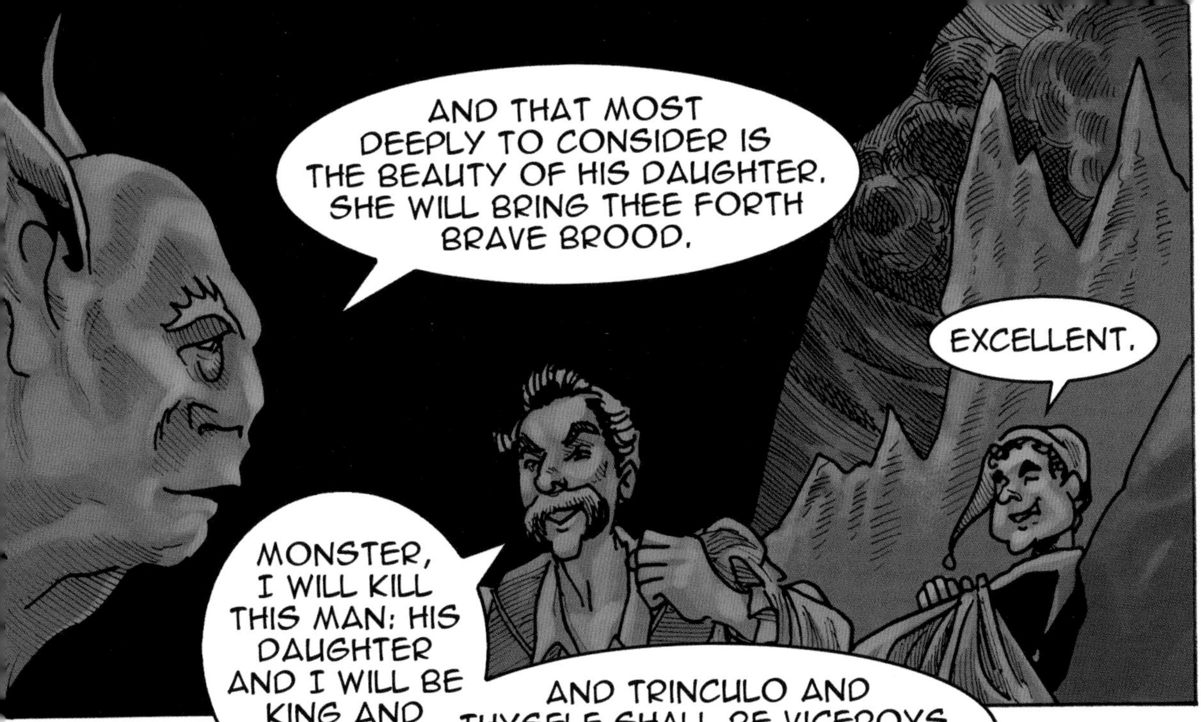
AND THAT MOST DEEPLY TO CONSIDER IS THE BEAUTY OF HIS DAUGHTER. SHE WILL BRING THEE FORTH BRAVE BROOD.
EXCELLENT.
MONSTER, I WILL KILL THIS MAN: HIS DAUGHTER AND I WILL BE KING AND QUEEN!
AND TRINCULO AND THYSELF SHALL BE VICEROYS. DOST THOU LIKE THAT PLOT, TRINCULO?

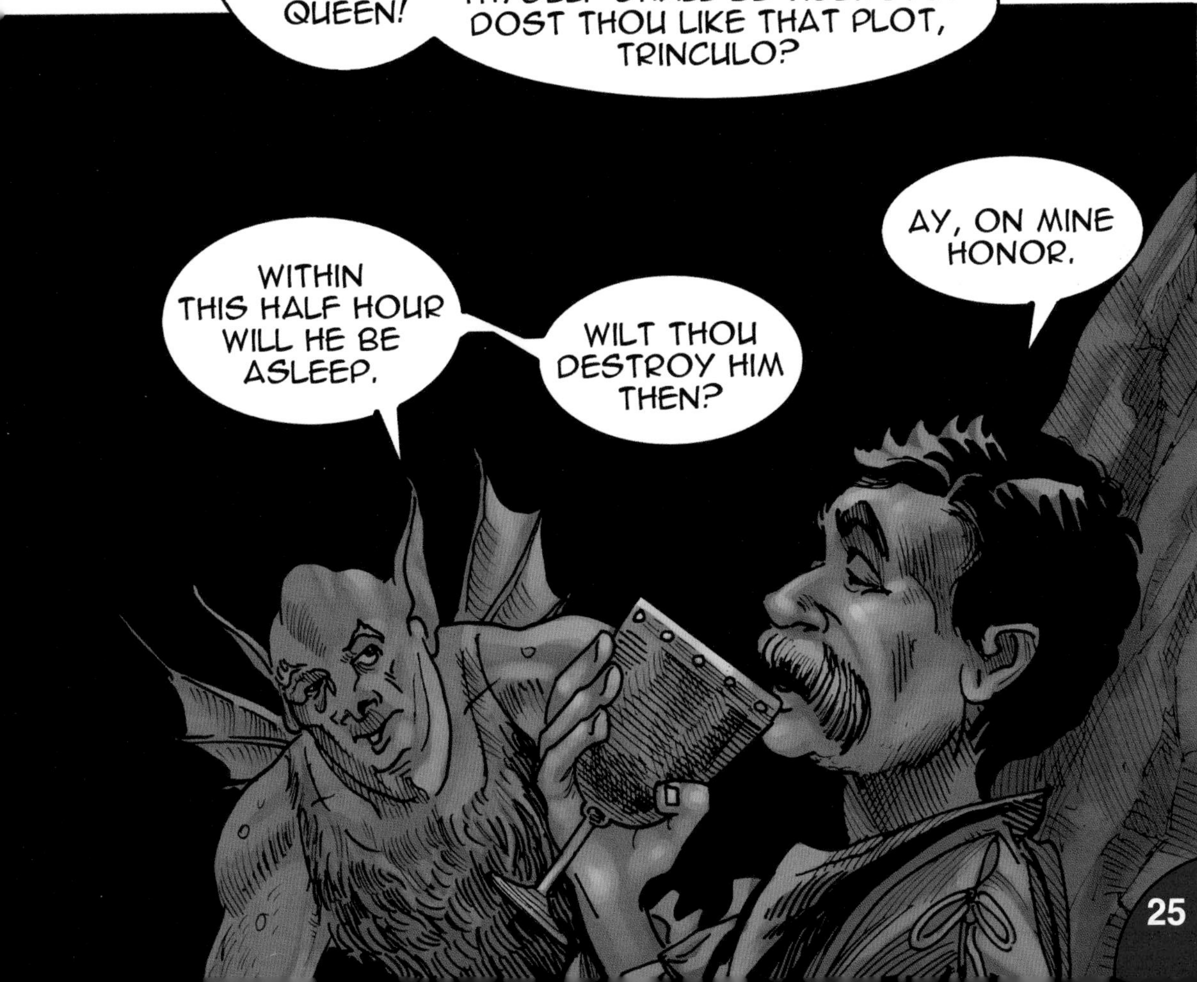
AY, ON MINE HONOR.
WITHIN THIS HALF HOUR WILL HE BE ASLEEP.
WILT THOU DESTROY HIM THEN?

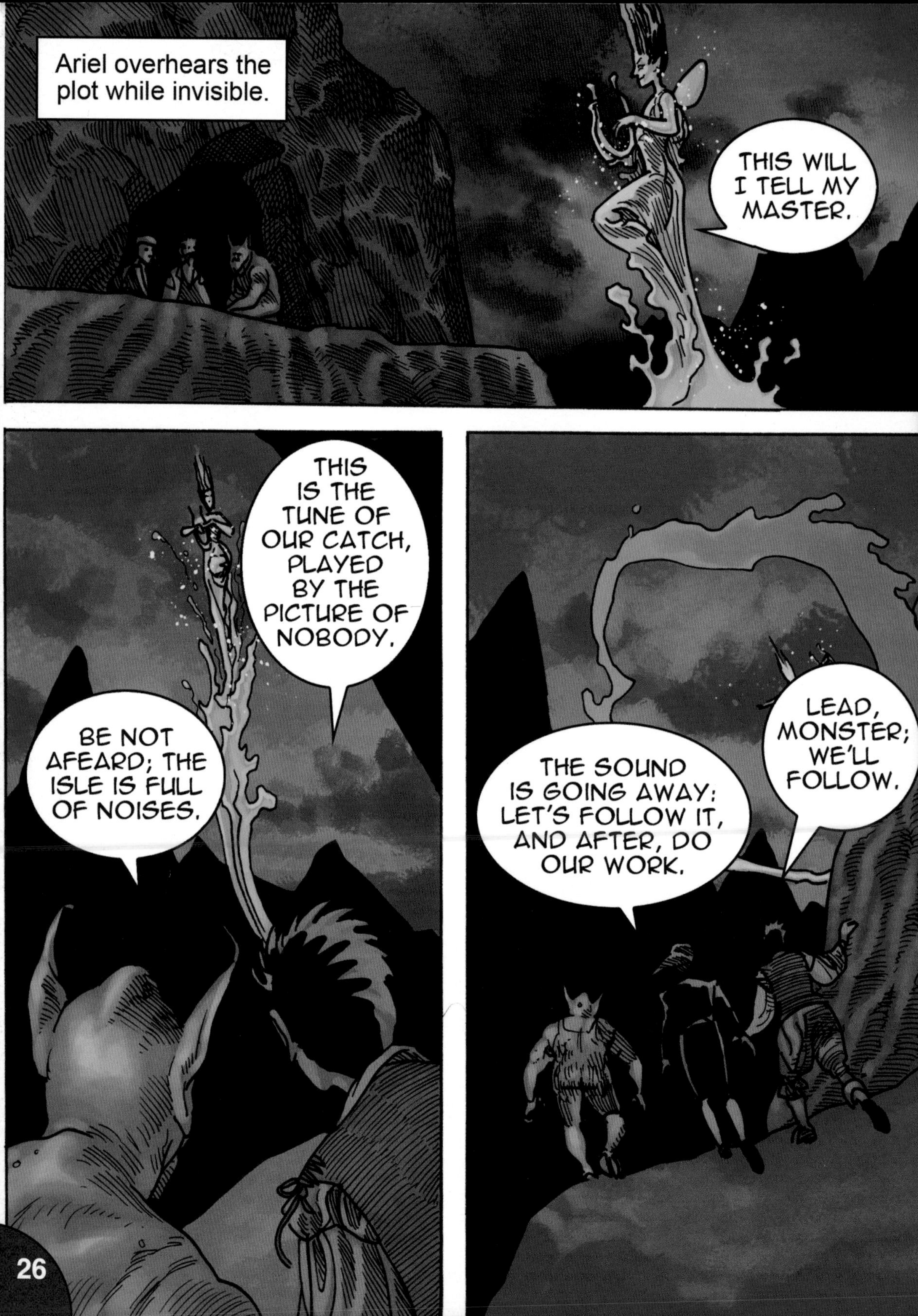
Ariel overhears the plot while invisible.
THIS WILL I TELL MY MASTER.
THIS IS THE TUNE OF OUR CATCH, PLAYED BY THE PICTURE OF NOBODY.
BE NOT AFEARD; THE ISLE IS FULL OF NOISES.
THE SOUND IS GOING AWAY: LET'S FOLLOW IT, AND AFTER, DO OUR WORK.
LEAD, MONSTER; WE'LL FOLLOW.

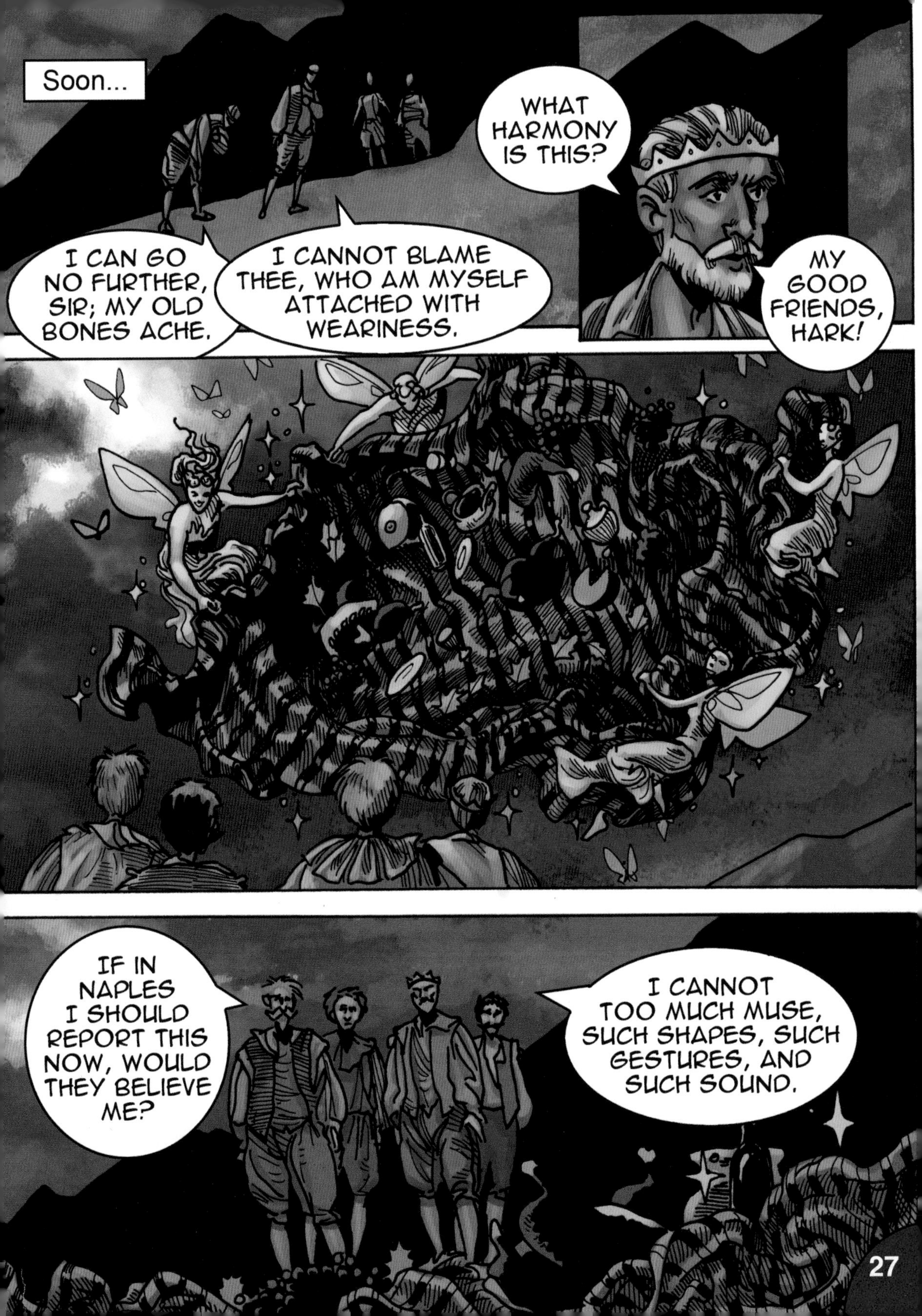
Soon...
I CAN GO NO FURTHER, SIR; MY OLD BONES ACHE.
I CANNOT BLAME THEE, WHO AM MYSELF ATTACHED WITH WEARINESS.
WHAT HARMONY IS THIS?
MY GOOD FRIENDS, HARK!
IF IN NAPLES I SHOULD REPORT THIS NOW, WOULD THEY BELIEVE ME?
I CANNOT TOO MUCH MUSE, SUCH SHAPES, SUCH GESTURES, AND SUCH SOUND.

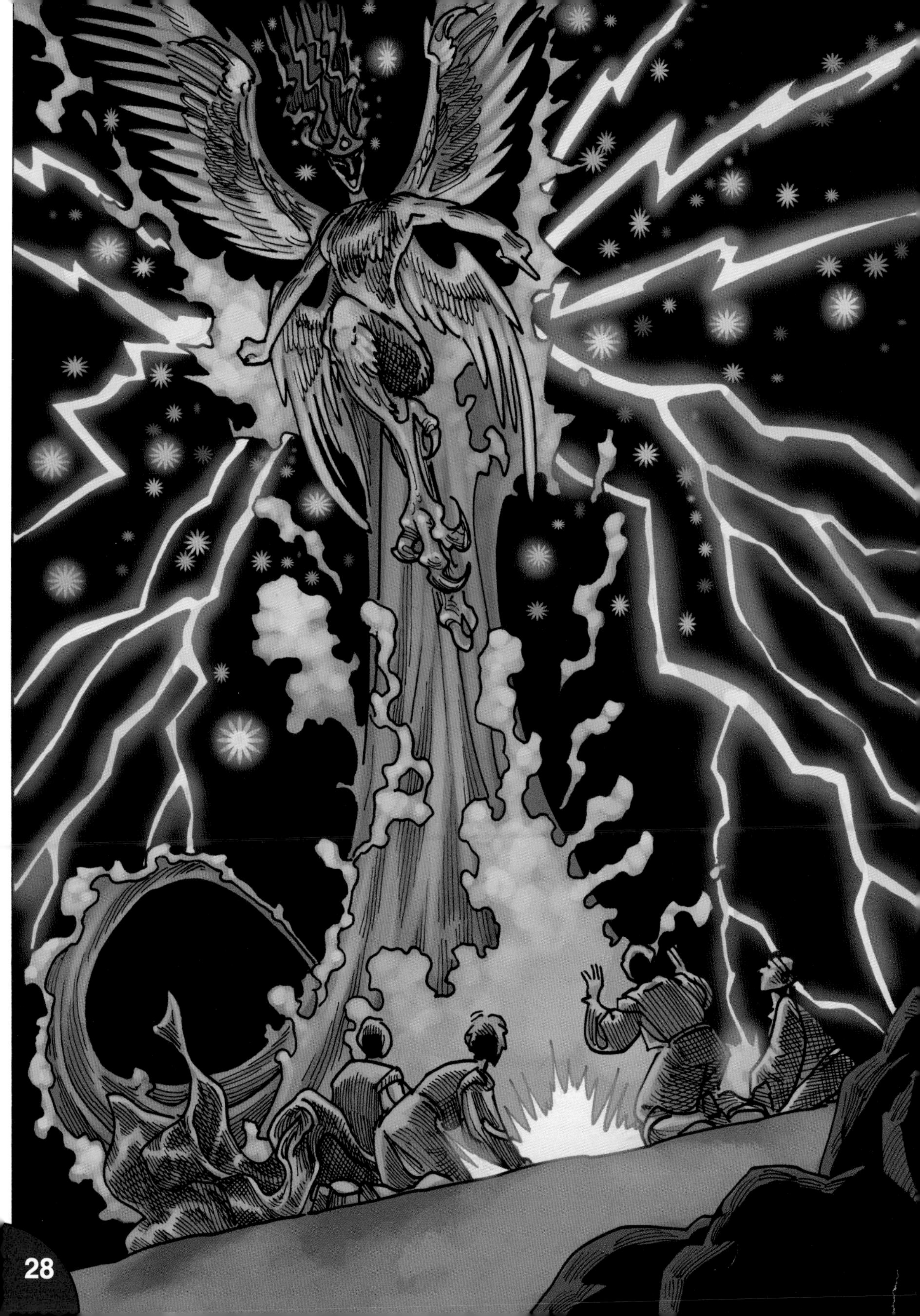

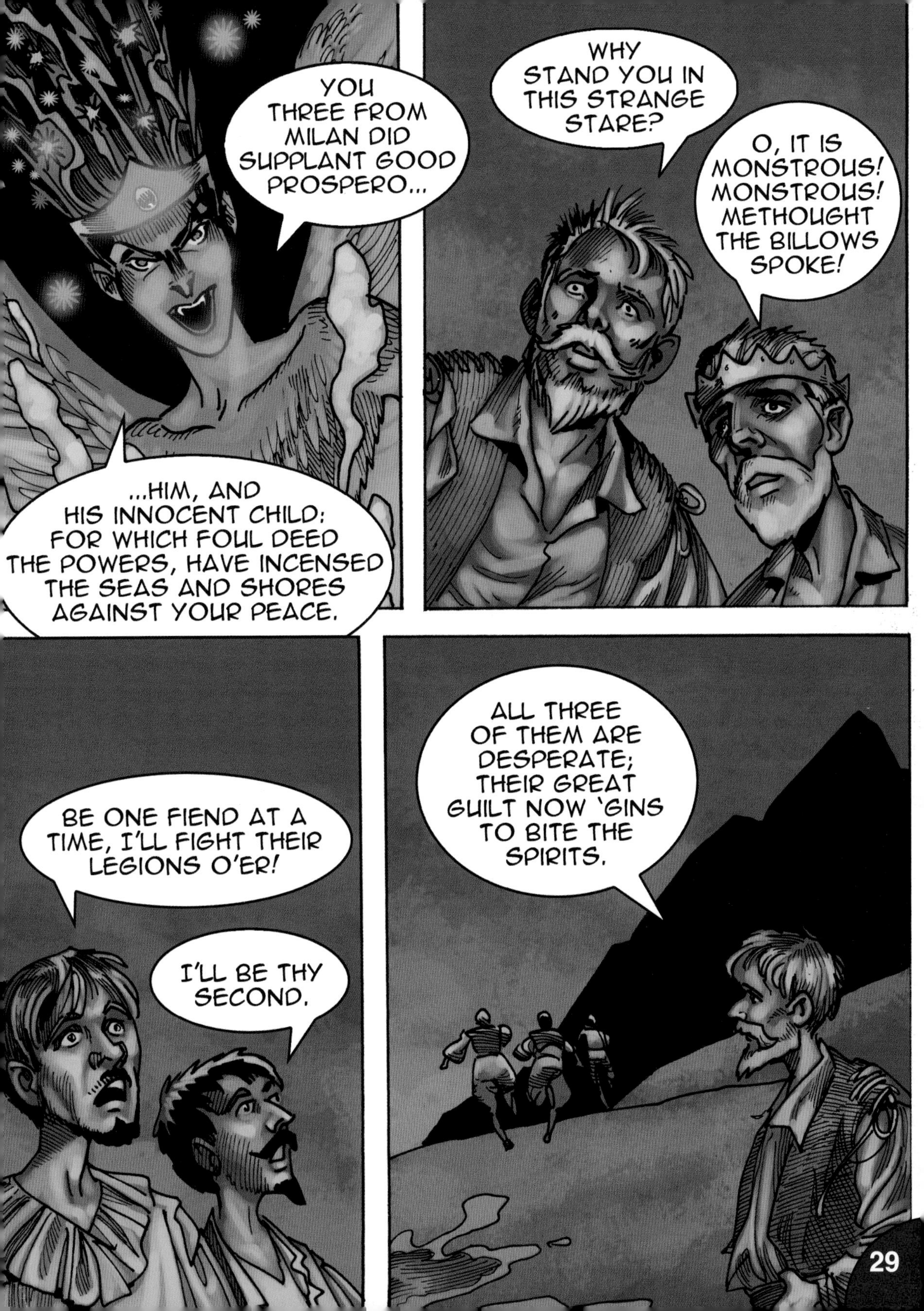
YOU THREE FROM MILAN DID SUPPLANT GOOD PROSPERO...
...HIM, AND HIS INNOCENT CHILD: FOR WHICH FOUL DEED THE POWERS, HAVE INCENSED THE SEAS AND SHORES AGAINST YOUR PEACE.
WHY STAND YOU IN THIS STRANGE STARE?
O, IT IS MONSTROUS! MONSTROUS! METHOUGHT THE BILLOWS SPOKE!
BE ONE FIEND AT A TIME, I'LL FIGHT THEIR LEGIONS O'ER!
I'LL BE THY SECOND.
ALL THREE OF THEM ARE DESPERATE; THEIR GREAT GUILT NOW 'GINS TO BITE THE SPIRITS.

Act IV

Prospero has decided to allow Miranda and Ferdinand to marry.

...FOR I HAVE GIVEN YOU HERE A THIRD OF MY OWN LIFE.

IF I HAVE TOO AUSTERELY PUNISHED YOU, YOUR COMPENSATION MAKES AMENDS...

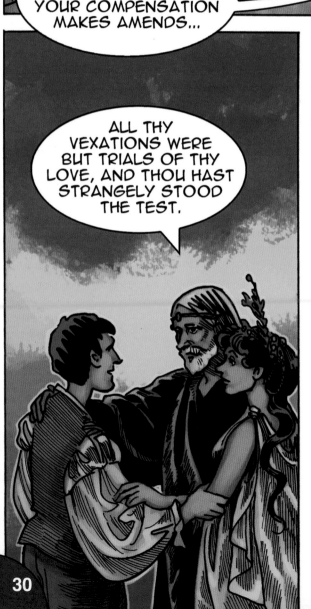

ALL THY VEXATIONS WERE BUT TRIALS OF THY LOVE, AND THOU HAST STRANGELY STOOD THE TEST.

ARIEL! GO BRING THE RABBLE, O'ER WHOM I GIVE THEE POW'R.

FOR I MUST BESTOW UPON THE EYES OF THIS YOUNG COUPLE SOME VANITY OF MINE ART.

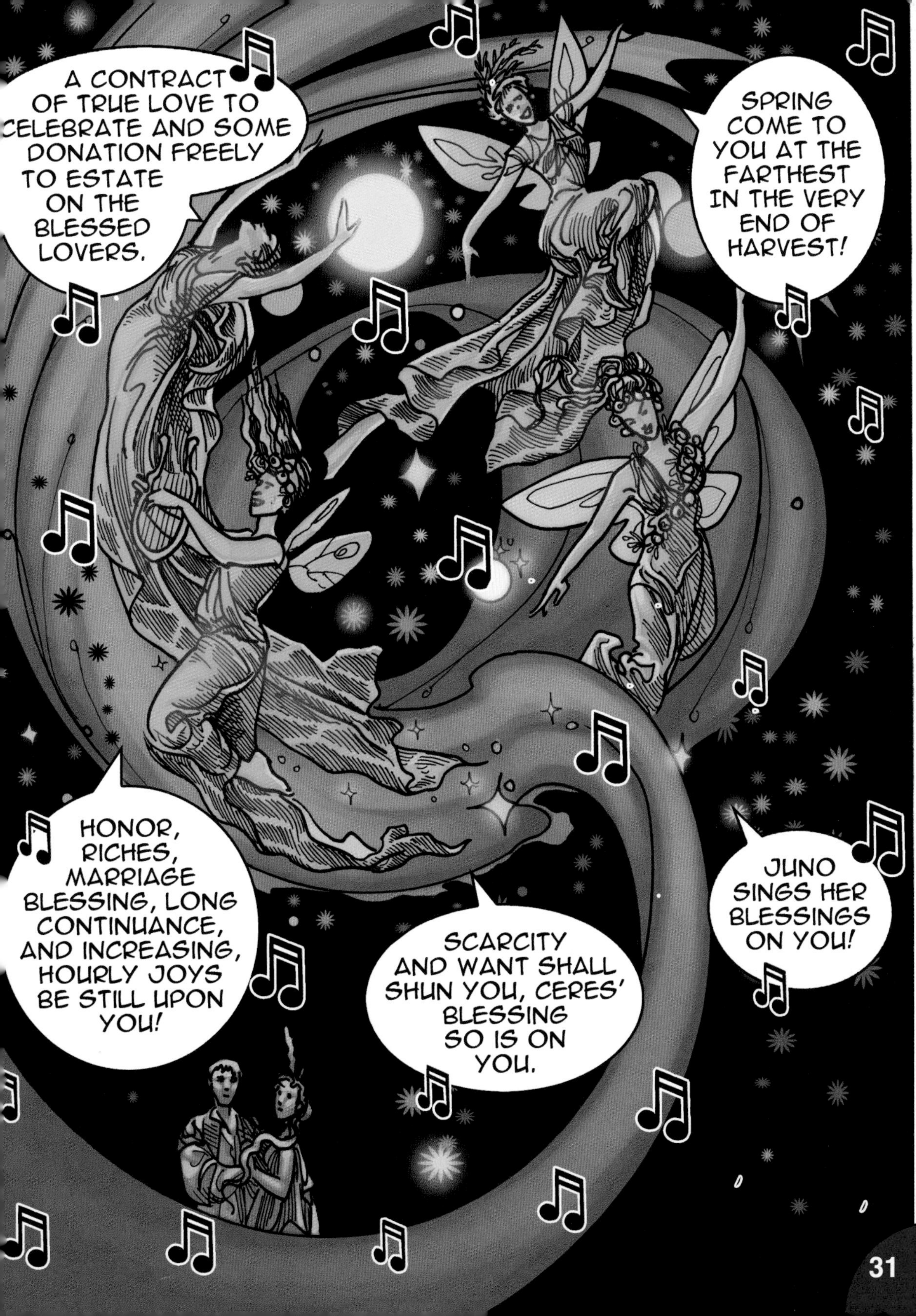

A CONTRACT OF TRUE LOVE TO CELEBRATE AND SOME DONATION FREELY TO ESTATE ON THE BLESSED LOVERS.
SPRING COME TO YOU AT THE FARTHEST IN THE VERY END OF HARVEST!
HONOR, RICHES, MARRIAGE BLESSING, LONG CONTINUANCE, AND INCREASING, HOURLY JOYS BE STILL UPON YOU!
SCARCITY AND WANT SHALL SHUN YOU, CERES' BLESSING SO IS ON YOU.
JUNO SINGS HER BLESSINGS ON YOU!

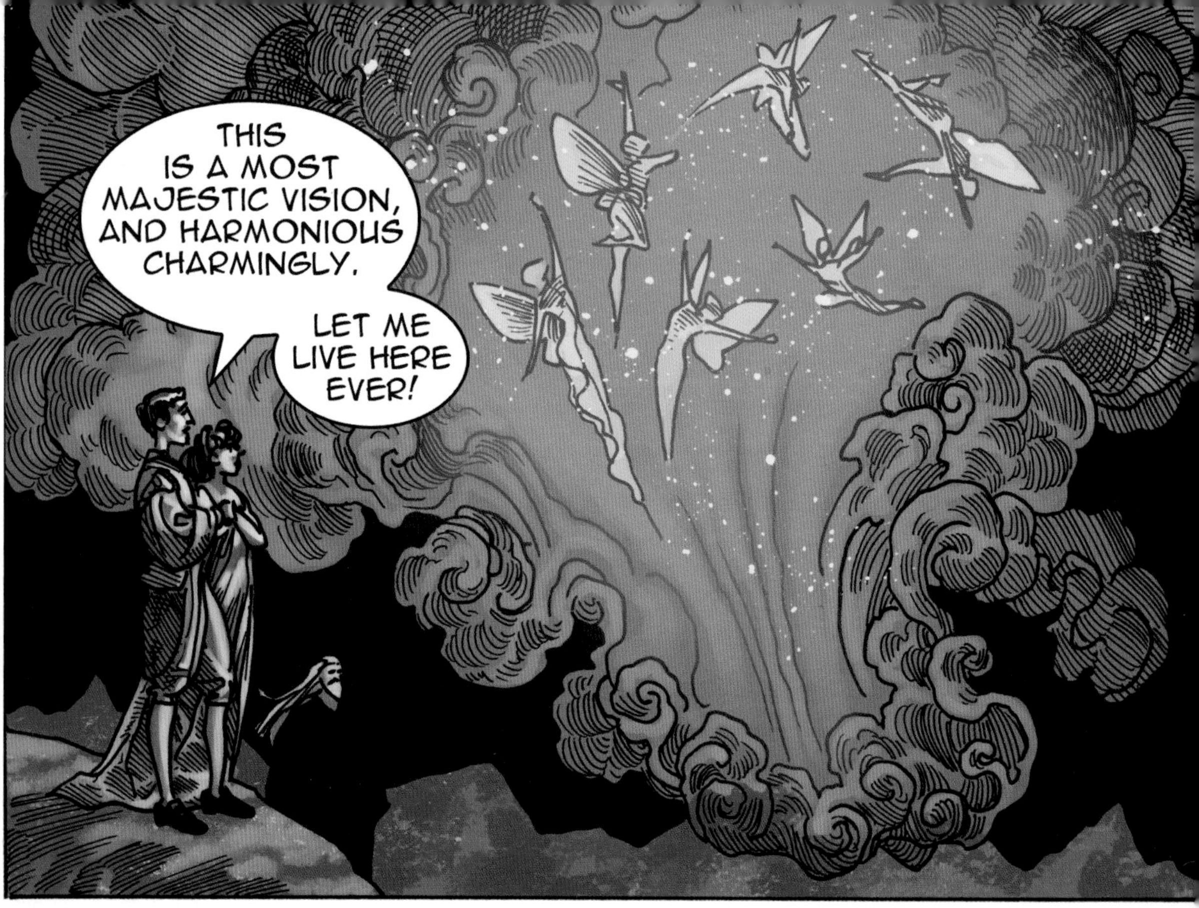
THIS IS A MOST MAJESTIC VISION, AND HARMONIOUS CHARMINGLY.
LET ME LIVE HERE EVER!

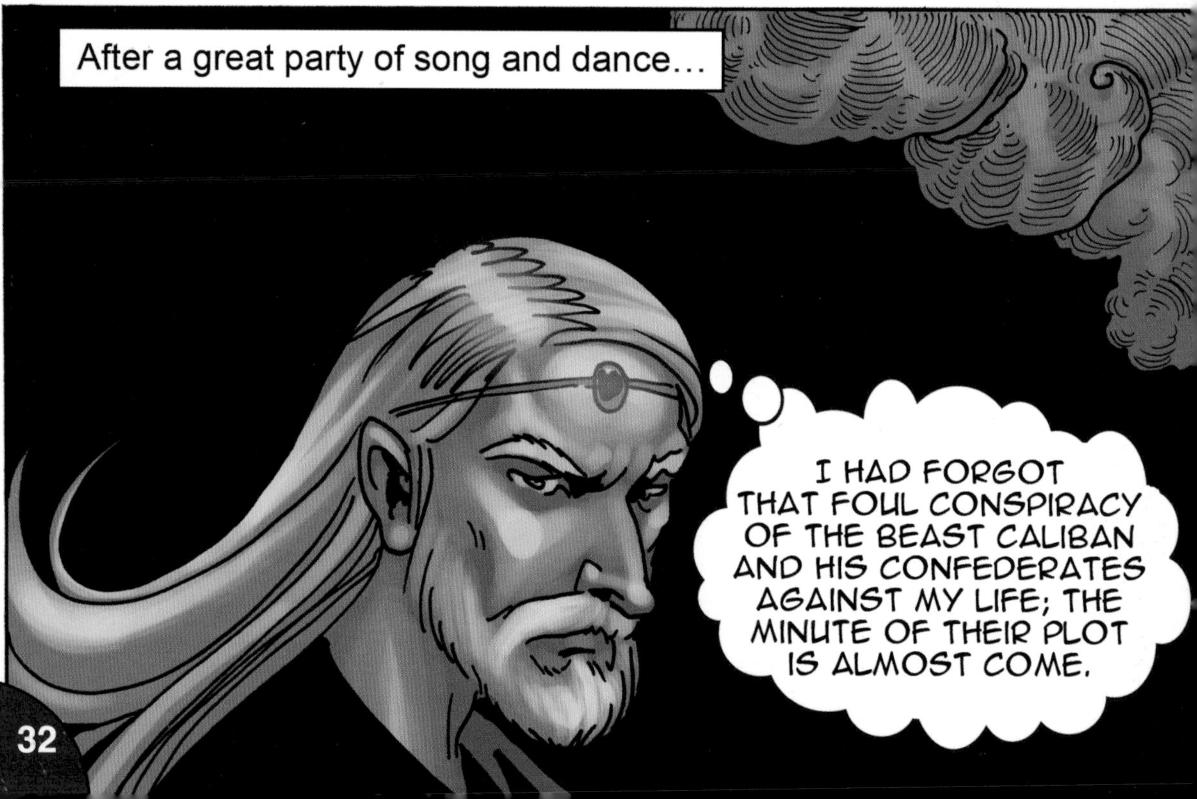
After a great party of song and dance…
I HAD FORGOT THAT FOUL CONSPIRACY OF THE BEAST CALIBAN AND HIS CONFEDERATES AGAINST MY LIFE; THE MINUTE OF THEIR PLOT IS ALMOST COME.

I THANK THEE, ARIEL. COME.

SPIRIT, WE MUST PREPARE TO MEET WITH CALIBAN.

WHAT'S THY PLEASURE?

THY SHAPE INVISIBLE RETAIN THOU STILL.

THE TRUMPERY IN MY HOUSE, GO BRING IT HITHER.

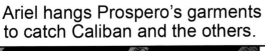

Ariel hangs Prospero's garments to catch Caliban and the others.

O WORTHY STEPHANO, LOOK WHAT A WARDROBE HERE IS FOR THEE.

BY THIS HAND, I'LL HAVE THAT GOWN!

SEEST THOU HERE? THIS IS THE MOUTH O' THE CELL.

DO THAT GOOD MISCHIEF, WHICH MAY MAKE THIS ISLAND THINE OWN FOREVER.

GIVE ME THY HAND. I DO BEGIN TO HAVE BLOODY THOUGHTS.

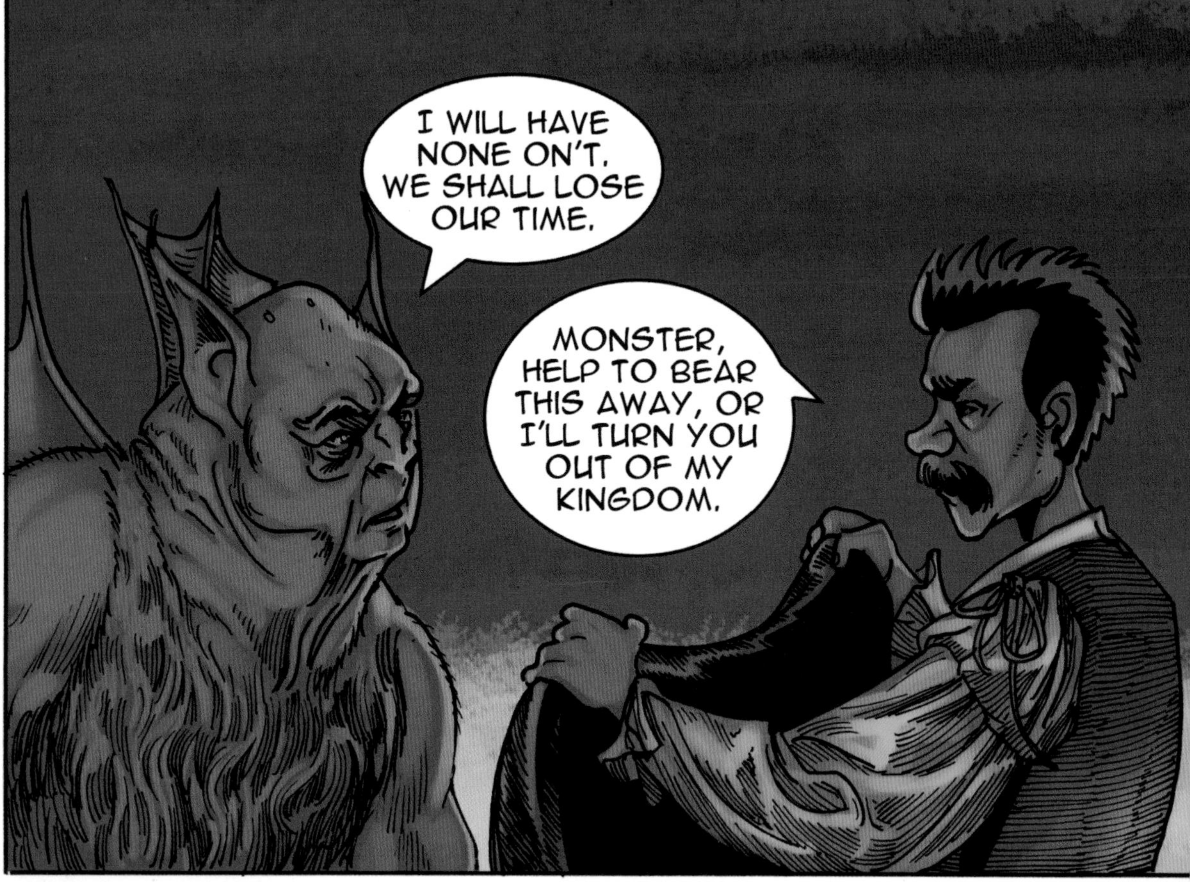
I WILL HAVE NONE ON'T. WE SHALL LOSE OUR TIME.
MONSTER, HELP TO BEAR THIS AWAY, OR I'LL TURN YOU OUT OF MY KINGDOM.

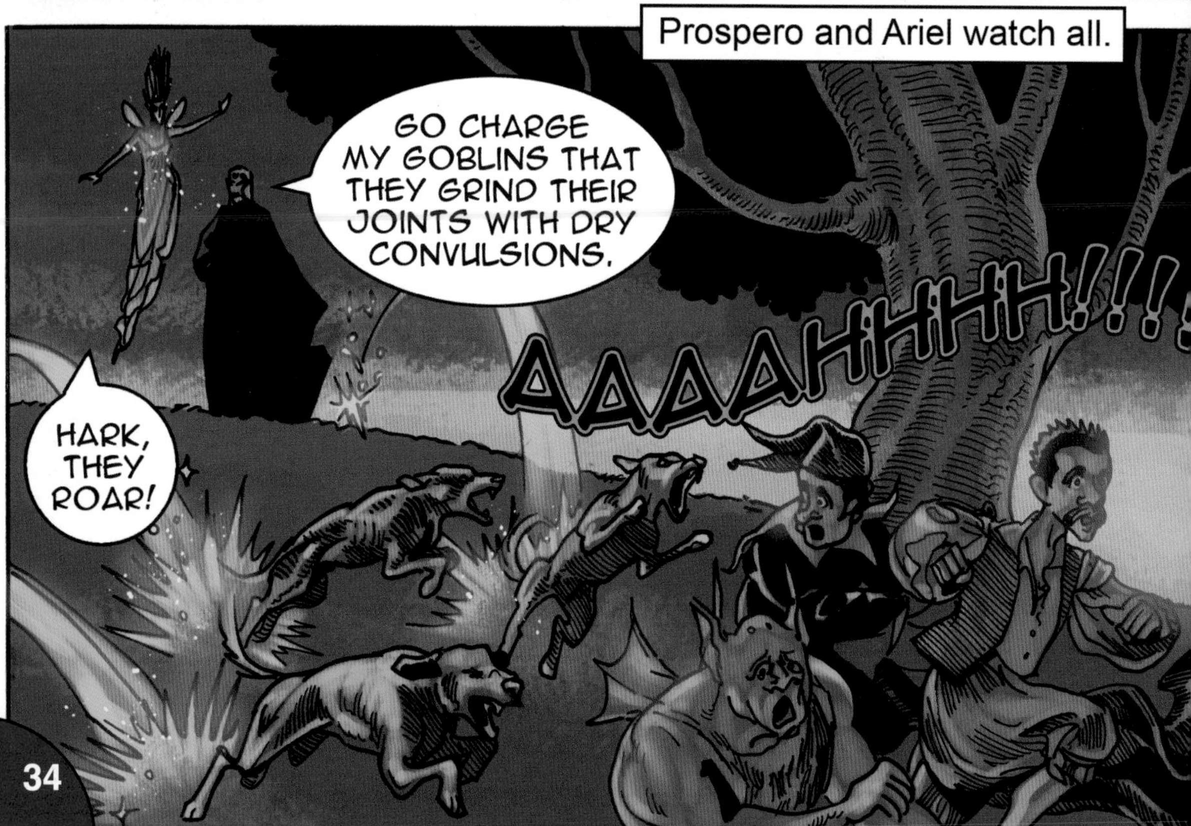
Prospero and Ariel watch all.
GO CHARGE MY GOBLINS THAT THEY GRIND THEIR JOINTS WITH DRY CONVULSIONS.
HARK, THEY ROAR!
AAAAHHHHHH!!!!

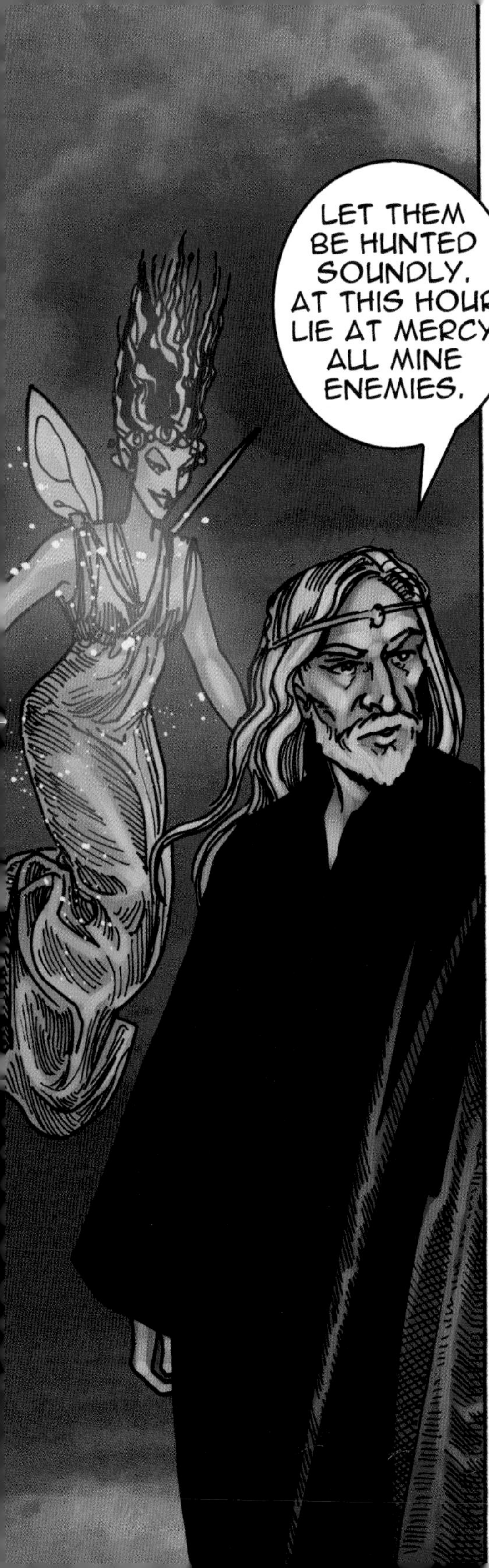
LET THEM BE HUNTED SOUNDLY. AT THIS HOUR LIE AT MERCY ALL MINE ENEMIES.

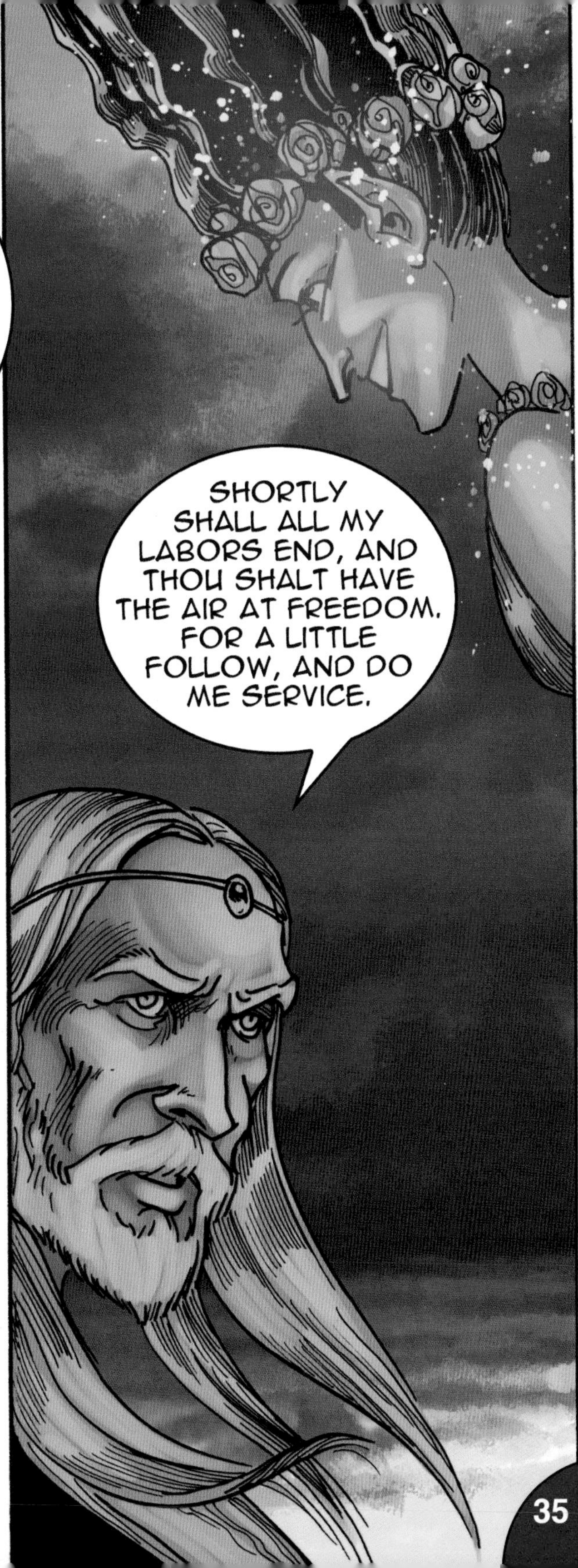
SHORTLY SHALL ALL MY LABORS END, AND THOU SHALT HAVE THE AIR AT FREEDOM. FOR A LITTLE FOLLOW, AND DO ME SERVICE.

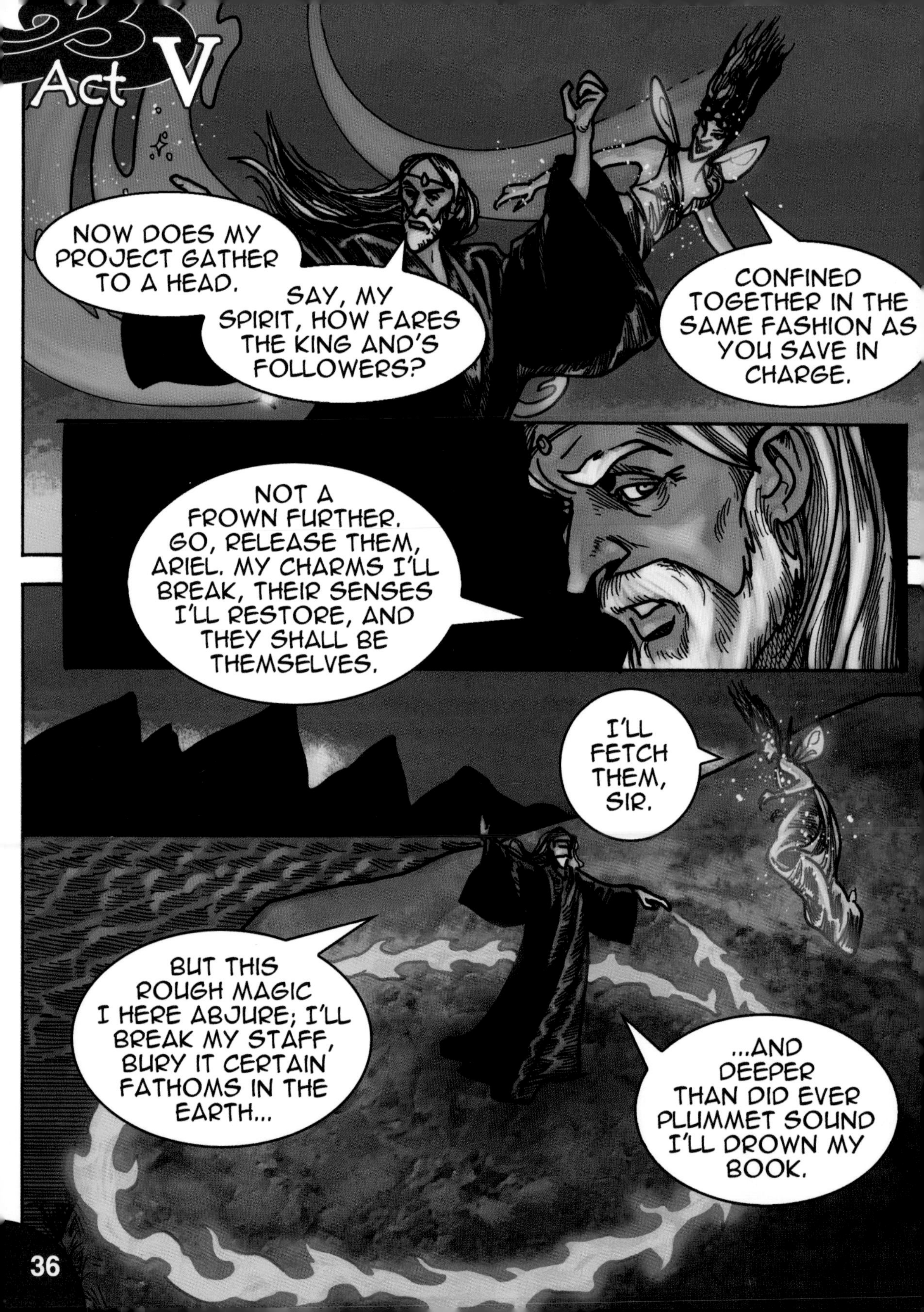
Act V
NOW DOES MY PROJECT GATHER TO A HEAD.
SAY, MY SPIRIT, HOW FARES THE KING AND'S FOLLOWERS?
CONFINED TOGETHER IN THE SAME FASHION AS YOU SAVE IN CHARGE.
NOT A FROWN FURTHER. GO, RELEASE THEM, ARIEL. MY CHARMS I'LL BREAK, THEIR SENSES I'LL RESTORE, AND THEY SHALL BE THEMSELVES.
I'LL FETCH THEM, SIR.
BUT THIS ROUGH MAGIC I HERE ABJURE; I'LL BREAK MY STAFF, BURY IT CERTAIN FATHOMS IN THE EARTH...
...AND DEEPER THAN DID EVER PLUMMET SOUND I'LL DROWN MY BOOK.

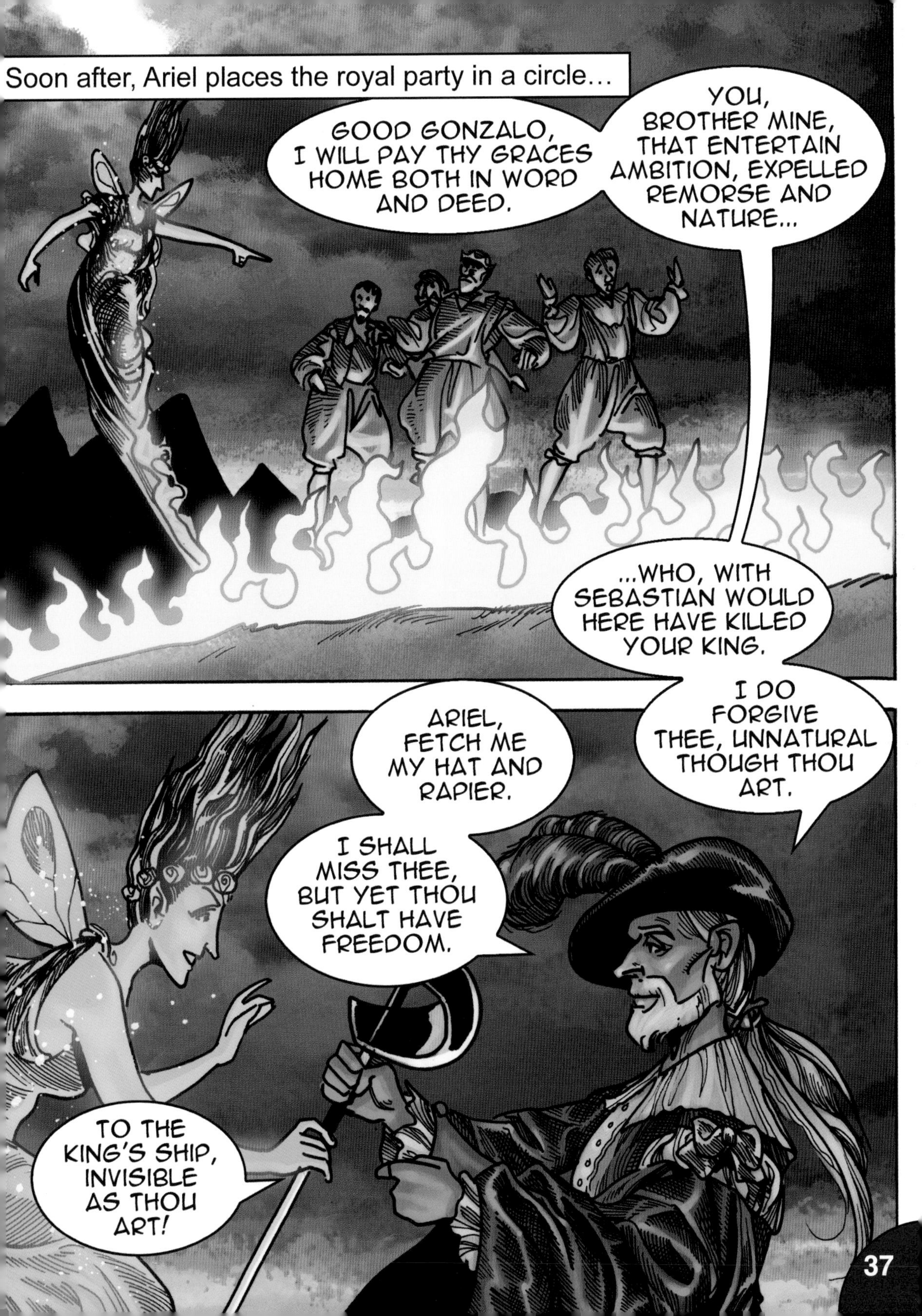

Soon after, Ariel places the royal party in a circle…
GOOD GONZALO, I WILL PAY THY GRACES HOME BOTH IN WORD AND DEED.
YOU, BROTHER MINE, THAT ENTERTAIN AMBITION, EXPELLED REMORSE AND NATURE...
...WHO, WITH SEBASTIAN WOULD HERE HAVE KILLED YOUR KING.
I DO FORGIVE THEE, UNNATURAL THOUGH THOU ART.
ARIEL, FETCH ME MY HAT AND RAPIER.
I SHALL MISS THEE, BUT YET THOU SHALT HAVE FREEDOM.
TO THE KING'S SHIP, INVISIBLE AS THOU ART!

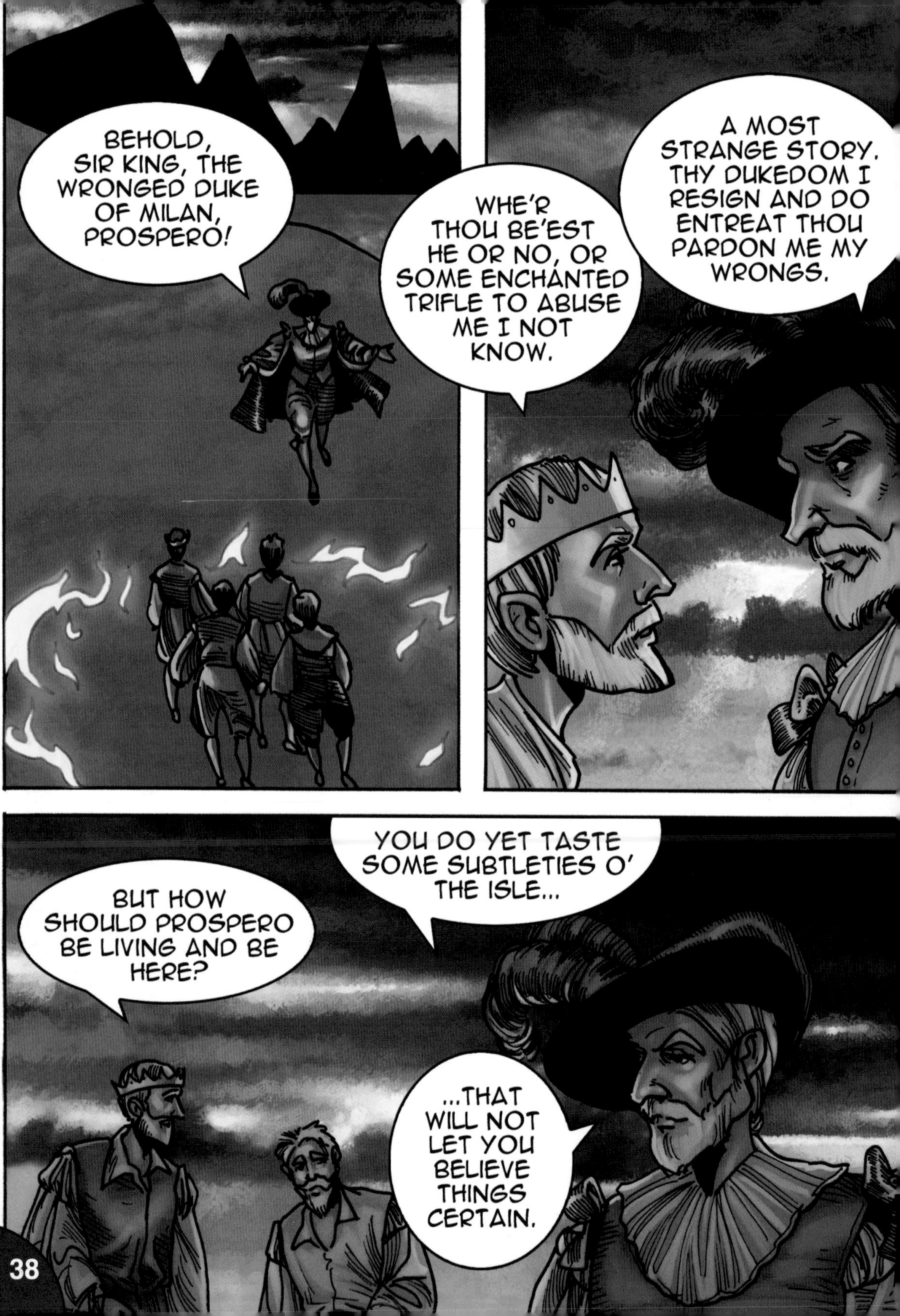
BEHOLD, SIR KING, THE WRONGED DUKE OF MILAN, PROSPERO!
WHE'R THOU BE'EST HE OR NO, OR SOME ENCHANTED TRIFLE TO ABUSE ME I NOT KNOW.
A MOST STRANGE STORY. THY DUKEDOM I RESIGN AND DO ENTREAT THOU PARDON ME MY WRONGS.
BUT HOW SHOULD PROSPERO BE LIVING AND BE HERE?
YOU DO YET TASTE SOME SUBTLETIES O' THE ISLE...
...THAT WILL NOT LET YOU BELIEVE THINGS CERTAIN.

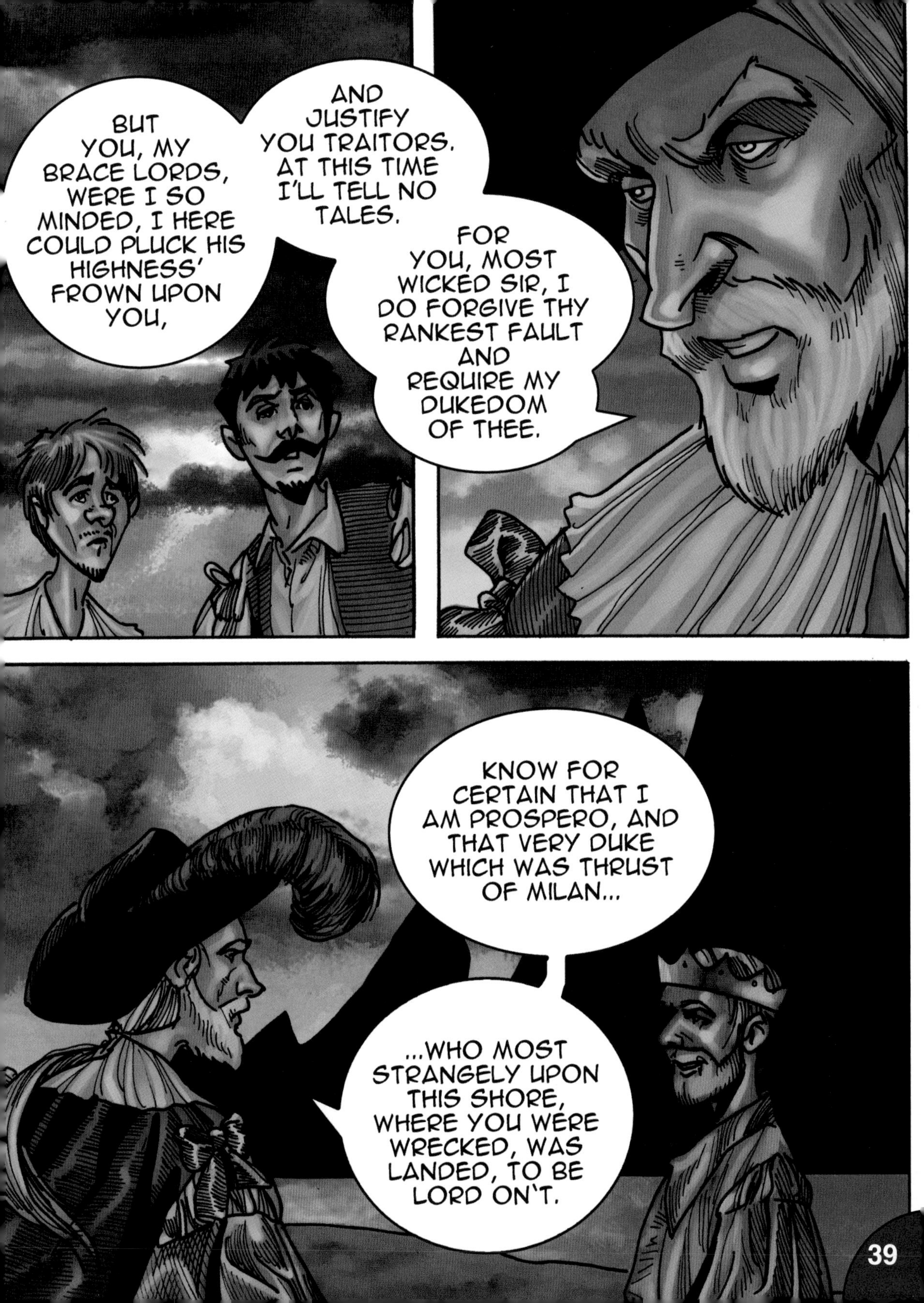
BUT YOU, MY BRACE LORDS, WERE I SO MINDED, I HERE COULD PLUCK HIS HIGHNESS' FROWN UPON YOU,
AND JUSTIFY YOU TRAITORS. AT THIS TIME I'LL TELL NO TALES.
FOR YOU, MOST WICKED SIR, I DO FORGIVE THY RANKEST FAULT AND REQUIRE MY DUKEDOM OF THEE.
KNOW FOR CERTAIN THAT I AM PROSPERO, AND THAT VERY DUKE WHICH WAS THRUST OF MILAN...
...WHO MOST STRANGELY UPON THIS SHORE, WHERE YOU WERE WRECKED, WAS LANDED, TO BE LORD ON'T.

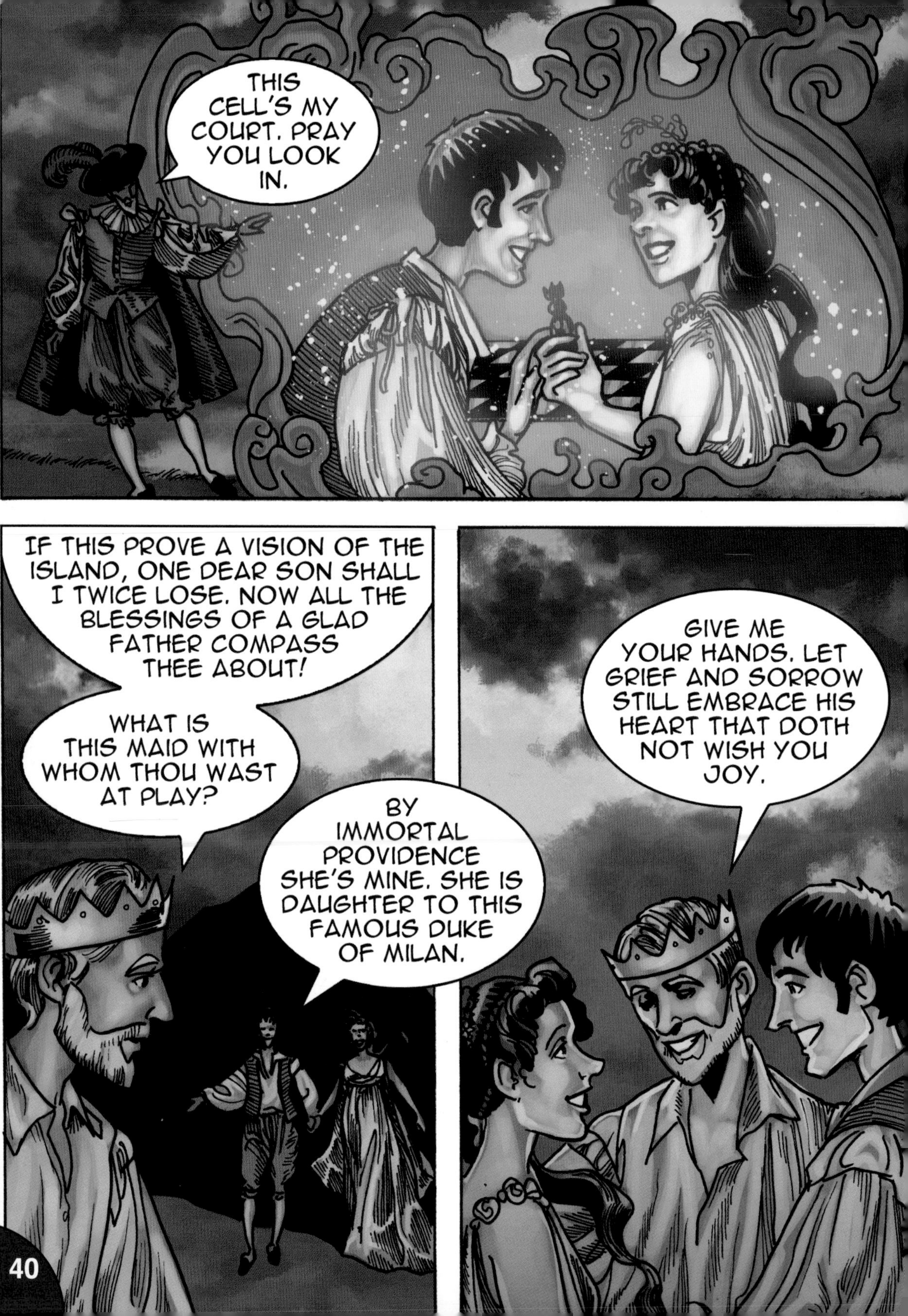
THIS CELL'S MY COURT. PRAY YOU LOOK IN.
IF THIS PROVE A VISION OF THE ISLAND, ONE DEAR SON SHALL I TWICE LOSE. NOW ALL THE BLESSINGS OF A GLAD FATHER COMPASS THEE ABOUT!
WHAT IS THIS MAID WITH WHOM THOU WAST AT PLAY?
BY IMMORTAL PROVIDENCE SHE'S MINE. SHE IS DAUGHTER TO THIS FAMOUS DUKE OF MILAN.
GIVE ME YOUR HANDS. LET GRIEF AND SORROW STILL EMBRACE HIS HEART THAT DOTH NOT WISH YOU JOY.

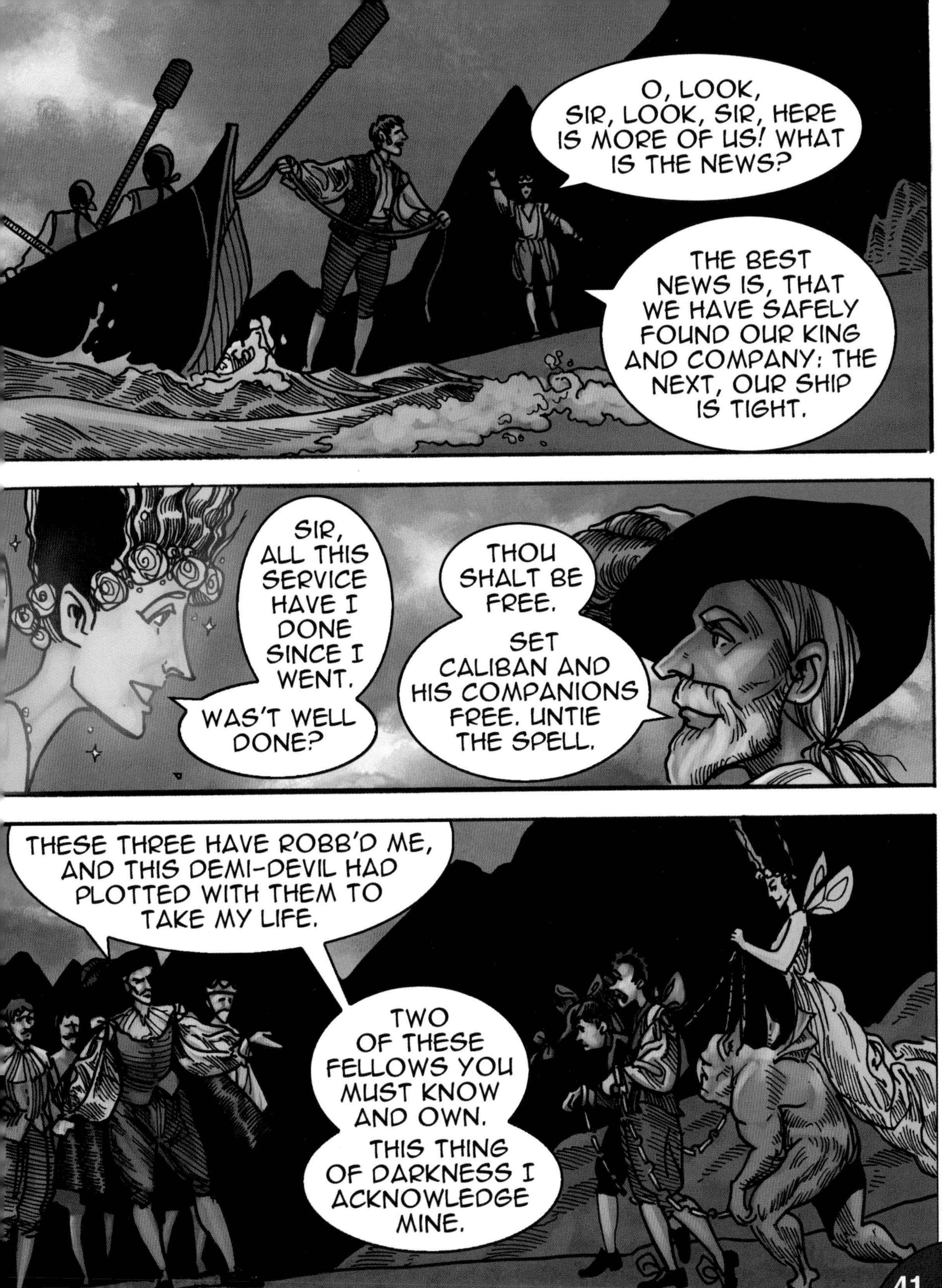
O, LOOK, SIR, LOOK, SIR, HERE IS MORE OF US! WHAT IS THE NEWS?
THE BEST NEWS IS, THAT WE HAVE SAFELY FOUND OUR KING AND COMPANY: THE NEXT, OUR SHIP IS TIGHT.
SIR, ALL THIS SERVICE HAVE I DONE SINCE I WENT.
WAS'T WELL DONE?
THOU SHALT BE FREE.
SET CALIBAN AND HIS COMPANIONS FREE. UNTIE THE SPELL.
THESE THREE HAVE ROBB'D ME, AND THIS DEMI-DEVIL HAD PLOTTED WITH THEM TO TAKE MY LIFE.
TWO OF THESE FELLOWS YOU MUST KNOW AND OWN.
THIS THING OF DARKNESS I ACKNOWLEDGE MINE.

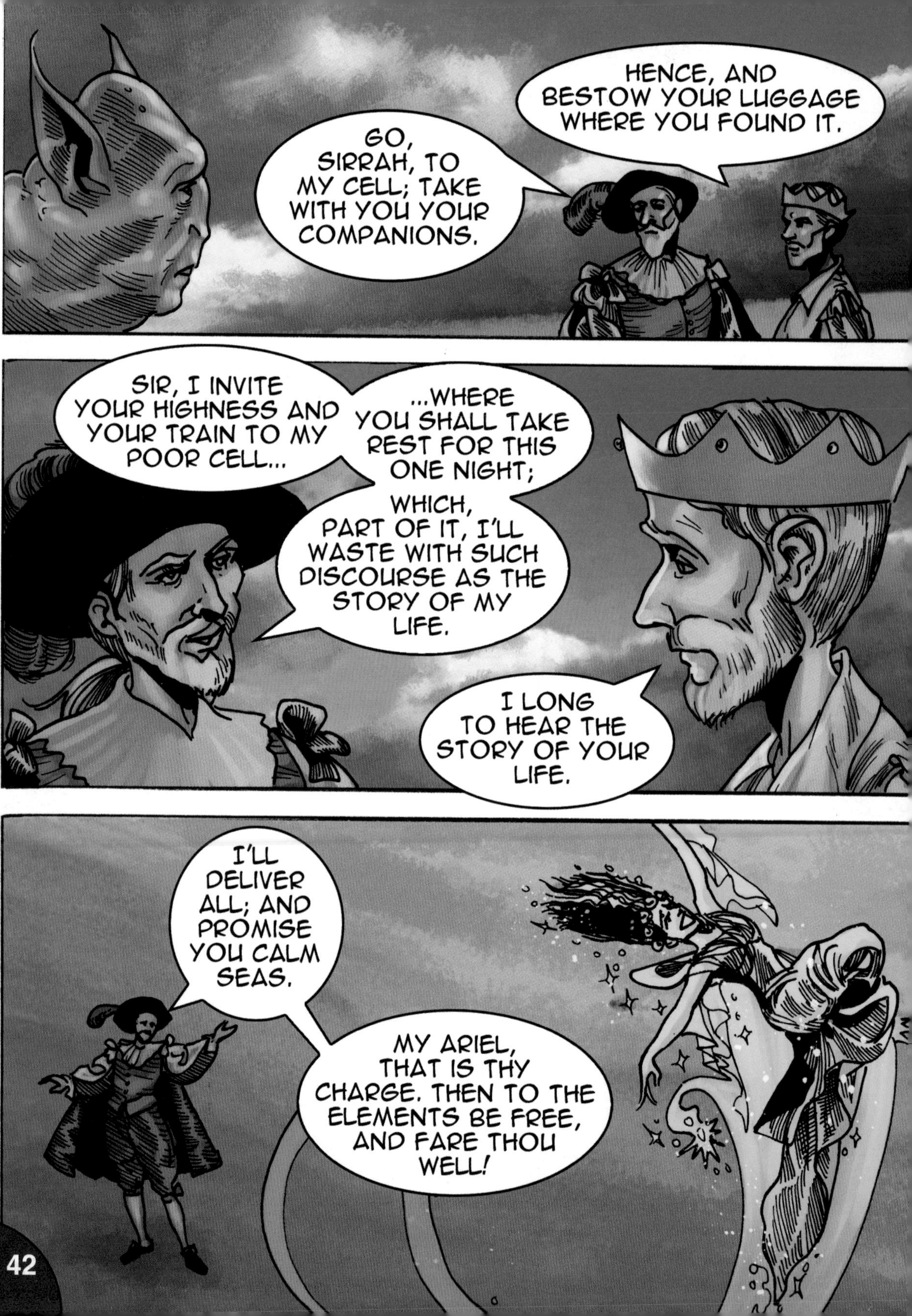
GO, SIRRAH, TO MY CELL; TAKE WITH YOU YOUR COMPANIONS.
HENCE, AND BESTOW YOUR LUGGAGE WHERE YOU FOUND IT.
SIR, I INVITE YOUR HIGHNESS AND YOUR TRAIN TO MY POOR CELL...
...WHERE YOU SHALL TAKE REST FOR THIS ONE NIGHT;
WHICH, PART OF IT, I'LL WASTE WITH SUCH DISCOURSE AS THE STORY OF MY LIFE.
I LONG TO HEAR THE STORY OF YOUR LIFE.
I'LL DELIVER ALL; AND PROMISE YOU CALM SEAS.
MY ARIEL, THAT IS THY CHARGE. THEN TO THE ELEMENTS BE FREE, AND FARE THOU WELL!

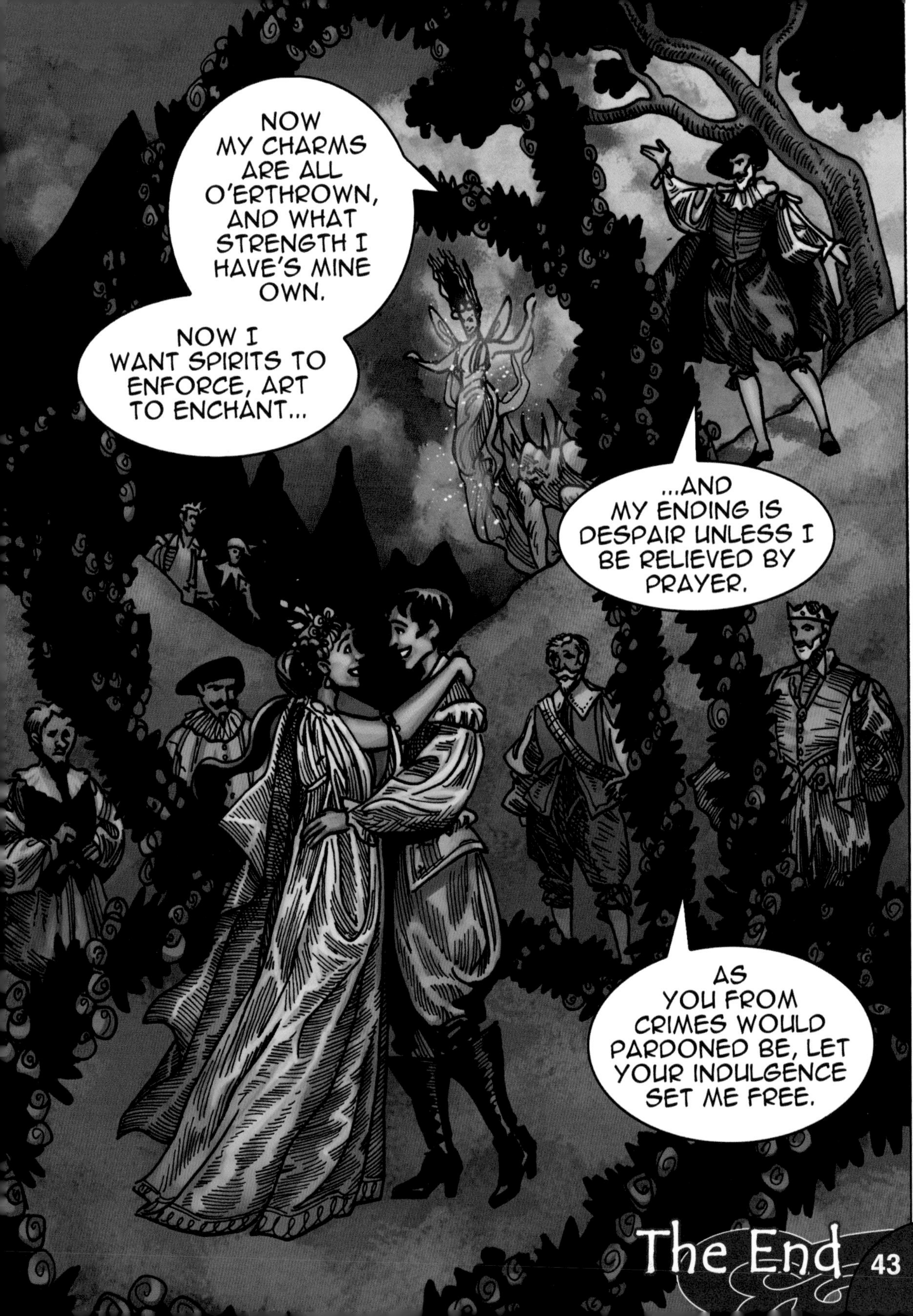
NOW MY CHARMS ARE ALL O'ERTHROWN, AND WHAT STRENGTH I HAVE'S MINE OWN.
NOW I WANT SPIRITS TO ENFORCE, ART TO ENCHANT...
...AND MY ENDING IS DESPAIR UNLESS I BE RELIEVED BY PRAYER.
AS YOU FROM CRIMES WOULD PARDONED BE, LET YOUR INDULGENCE SET ME FREE.
The End

Behind The Tempest

William Shakespeare wrote *The Tempest* in 1611. Shakespeare drew on stories of shipwrecks in the New World by English sailors for his play. The first performance of *The Tempest* was in 1611. The play was first published in 1623 in the collected works of Shakespeare called the *First Folio*. Today, the *First Folio* is the source for most of Shakespeare's plays.

The Tempest is set on a mystical island. The island lies near Italy, possibly in the Mediterranean Sea. The characters are from Italian cities of Milan and Naples. Both ancient cities were founded in 600 BC. They grew to be of great importance in Italy.

The play begins with a storm raised by Prospero. As Prospero and his daughter, Miranda, watch the storm, Prospero reveals that he is the rightful duke of Milan. He had been overthrown by his brother Antonio with Alonso, the king of Naples, and set adrift in the sea.

Prospero and Miranda were saved by the kindness of the serving man, Gonzalo. He had provided enough food and water for them to arrive on the island, where they had lived for the past 12 years. In that time, Prospero had used magic to free the sprite Ariel from imprisonment and take a slave in the native Caliban.

Prospero also reveals that he has raised the tempest to capture Antonio, Alonso, and Alonso's son, Ferdinand. However, he has Ariel separate them into three groups. Ariel also uses illusions so the king and his son each believe the other has died. Prospero and Ariel then watch the king's men as they try to survive on the island and plot the murders of Alonso and Prospero.

In the meantime, Ferdinand finds Prospero and Miranda. He instantly falls in love with Miranda and the couple is soon married. Prospero reconciles with Alonso and Antonio for his daughter's sake, and to make peace between Milan and Naples. Prospero sets Ariel and Caliban free, discards his magic, and returns safely to rule his kingdom.

Famous Phrases

Misery acquaints a man with strange bedfellows.

O brave new world that has such people in't!

We are such stuff as dreams are made on.

What's past is prologue.

What strength I have's mine own.

About the Author

William Shakespeare was baptized on April 26, 1564, in Stratford-upon-Avon, England. At the time, records were not kept of births, however, the churches did record baptisms, weddings, and deaths. So, we know approximately when he was born. Traditionally, his birth is celebrated on April 23.

William was the son of John Shakespeare, a tradesman, and Mary Arden. He most likely attended grammar school and learned to read, write, and speak Latin.

Shakespeare did not go on to the university. Instead, he married Anne Hathaway at age 18. They had three children, Susanna, Hamnet, and Judith. Not much is known about Shakespeare's life at this time. By 1592 he had moved to London, and his name began to appear in the literary world.

In 1594, Shakespeare became an important member of Lord Chamberlain's company of players. This group had the best actors and the best theater, the Globe. For the next 20 years, Shakespeare devoted himself to writing. He died on April 23, 1616, but his works have lived on.

Additional Works by Shakespeare

The Comedy of Errors (1589–94)
The Taming of the Shrew (1590–94)
Romeo and Juliet (1594–96)
A Midsummer Night's Dream (1595–96)
Much Ado About Nothing (1598–99)
As You Like It (1598–1600)
Hamlet (1599–1601)
Twelfth Night (1600–02)
Othello (1603–04)
King Lear (1605–06)
Macbeth (1606–07)
The Tempest (1611)

About the Adapters

Dan Conner is a high school teacher and small group leader at his church in San Antonio, TX, where he lives with his sensational wife, Hannah, and their cat. He is a lifelong comic book and literature fan, and so is thrilled to be a part of this Graphic Novel series. Other works of his, including musical endeavors, have appeared in various comic book anthologies, CDs, and websites.

Cynthia Martin is one of the few women working in mainstream American comics. She worked for Marvel, pencilling and inking several titles such as *Star Wars*. She also drew for the comic series *Elvira*, based on the television show.

Glossary

austerely - sternly.

bark - a small sailing ship.

Ceres - goddess of agriculture.

changed eyes - exchanged loving looks.

confederates - makes an alliance.

homage - expression of high regard.

incense - to excite or cause to happen.

inveterate - something that grew stronger over time.

league - a measurement of distance.

Neapolitan - a citizen of Naples.

perchance - by mere chance.

prithee - a way to make a request.

usurp - to take over by force.

viceroy - a representative of a king or queen.

Web Sites

To learn more about William Shakespeare, visit ABDO Publishing Company on the World Wide Web at **www.abdopublishing.com**. Web sites about Shakespeare are featured on our Book Links page. These links are routinely monitored and updated to provide the most current information available.